TAINTED

THE ARC SERIES BOOK ONE

ALEXANDRA MOODY

Copyright © 2017 by Alexandra Moody

All rights reserved.

No part of this book may be reproduced in any form or by any electronic or mechanical means, including information storage and retrieval systems, without written permission from the author, except for the use of brief quotations in a book review.

Edited by Pete Thompson
Cover Design by Alexandra Moody

ISBN-13: 978-1502916617
ISBN-10: 1502916614

For Mum and Dad.

CHAPTER ONE

There was a time when I was afraid of being tested. It wasn't the jab of the needle that scared me—that was nothing. Being taken away without any notice and without any goodbyes. Now, *that* was something to fear.

It's been years since I've worried about my annual testing. When you've lost as many people as I have, you come to terms with the possibility you too might be found tainted and taken away—but today is different.

I look down at the glass cuff that encases my wrist and my heartbeat quickens as I see the time. It's later than I thought. Only twenty minutes until the appointment now.

I rip my gaze away from the glowing blue numbers displayed across the CommuCuff's surface and attempt to focus on Ms. Matthews, who looks more like a relic of history than a teacher of it. She paces in front of the whiteboard, lecturing on the day of impact yet again.

You wouldn't think it'd be necessary to teach us about the asteroid that doomed us all. It's fairly safe to say after living down here in the ARC for fifteen years we've all become experts. Yet, there she stands critically breaking down the social ramifications of forcing a select few people from society down into a fallout shelter. God, I hope there isn't another test on this.

As I listen to the sound of Ms. Matthews' voice, I try to remind myself I'm not scared; that I'm not afraid and everything's going to be okay. It's no use. The courage I usually feel before my testing is gone and I'm completely consumed by fear. Then again, today is the exception. It's not me that's about to be tested, but Quinn.

I hazard another look at my cuff. Just fifteen minutes now. Fifteen minutes until Quinn's name is called out. Fifteen minutes until she's led into a cold, sterile room where her blood will be taken. If the result comes back clear, I'll see her at the end of the day. If not —if she's tainted ... I'll never see her again.

The thought causes shivers to run down my spine and I shake my head slightly, as if to rattle out the dark ideas that fill my mind. She's going to be okay. She has to be...

'*Elle!*' I turn to the sound of my name being irritably whispered from beside me. Amy Lau lifts her eyebrows at me and I follow the direction of her stare down to the stylus I restlessly tap against my desk.

'Sorry,' I whisper back to her, ceasing the patter.

I place the pen flat on the table and allow my fingers to drift up and play with the teardrop pearl pendant that hangs from the tarnished silver necklace I always wear. It's the one possession I have from before impact. I like to think it belonged to my parents—but I really wouldn't know.

A despondent sigh escapes my mouth. *It's no use.* I can't stop thinking about it—about her. About losing the closest thing I have to family in this run-down, worn-out fallout shelter.

I pick the stylus up and start tapping it against the table again. Tap, tap, tap, it drums against the wood. As I watch its quick successive raps, the edges of my vision flicker and the tarnished white walls of the classroom seem to warp.

I try to ignore the apprehension building inside of me. I can feel my hands getting clammy though, and an invisible oppressive mass seems to weigh down on my chest. My eyes dart frantically around the room, trying to find relief from this feeling of being trapped, but the door is closed and, of course, there are no windows.

I become intensely aware of the weight of the earth piled above me. The countless meters of dirt, rock and concrete I sit below. I tug at the neck of my top in an attempt to cool myself down.

Tap, tap, tap, the pen beats faster.

My peripheral vision can't ignore the tired walls as they gradually press inwards. I try to focus on the pen. The room is *not* getting smaller.

Beads of sweat trickle down the back of my neck, and my heart pounds so wildly in my chest my whole body shakes to the beat of its escalating thud.

I bow my head down and stare at the tablet on my desk. The words are a blur on the screen. *It's not real. The walls are not closing in.* Shutting my eyes, I concentrate on the sound of my soft, uneven breath, wheezing in and then rapidly rushing out again.

Get a grip Elle. You've been here nearly your entire life and the ARC hasn't caved in yet. I repeat this to myself over and over as I take more long, drawn-out breaths in and out, in and out.

Gradually my mind becomes clearer and the fear begins to recede. I push it back into the small, murky corner of my brain where it always lurks. I've kept it under control for so many years.

How easily it comes back.

It's laughable to think anyone who lives in the ARC could have a fear of being trapped. However, it's something I have struggled with for the last fifteen years, ever since the day of impact forced us to retreat underground.

'Seriously Elle!' Amy whispers in my ear, snapping me back to reality. I apologise to her again, immediately stopping the patter and lifting the stylus up to my mouth to chew on the end of it.

It would've been so easy for Quinn to give me her usual winsome smile at breakfast this morning. To say her testing would be over and done with before I knew it, and she'd see me back at our quarters tonight. Yes, that would've been so easy. *Too easy* it would seem.

She had been sitting across from me in the dining hall, stirring circles in her untouched porridge. She was withdrawn and nothing like her irritatingly perky self.

As much as I'd been concerned by her weird behaviour, what disturbed me the most hadn't been the way she acted. It had been what she said. Well, at least, what I think she said. It had been muttered so quietly, I hadn't been certain at the time I'd even heard it correctly. Hell, I hope I hadn't heard it correctly.

'*Can't be tainted if you don't get tested.*' Quinn's voice echoes through my thoughts again. Surely she won't try and hide...

I chew even harder on the end of my stylus. If she follows through on what I think I heard her planning, she could end up going before the Council. Would she really be stupid enough to risk that?

'Elle!' Amy kicks my leg under the table.

'Ouch. What?' I whisper back.

She nods her head to the front of the classroom where Ms. Matthews stares at me expectantly.

'Miss Winters?' she asks.

My gaze drops down to the tablet on my desk. I've completely missed everything she's said. 'Sorry, I—ah, didn't understand the question. Could you phrase it a different way?' I ask, hoping she hasn't noticed my complete lack of attention for the duration of her entire class.

Her face grows sterner. 'Maybe if you spent more time listening and less time daydreaming, you would not require my assistance in comprehending a basic question. You will attend detention for one hour at the conclusion of school today.'

'Yes Ms. Matthews,' I respond, attempting to keep the resentment from my voice. Of all the days to get detention, why does it have to be today?

My eyes unconsciously flicker towards Sebastian who's chatting easily with Kate. He catches me watching and turns his head slightly to roll his eyes at me. Kate's so busy talking about herself she doesn't even notice she's lost his attention for a moment.

I smile to myself and look away. Maybe he's not that riveted to her after all.

After another ten minutes of listening to Kate's ceaseless drivel, she finally leaves. I exhale a breath I didn't even know I was holding as I watch her perky behind strut its way to the door. When I look up I find Sebastian watching me. His eyes show concern, but I have no idea why. I squirm under his stare, uncomfortable with the intensity of his gaze.

'So, do you know what happened with Quinn today?' he eventually asks.

My stomach does a small flip as I think about her testing. 'No, I haven't heard anything,' I say quietly. 'It nearly killed me not being able to comm her during class, but even when I got out and tried there was no answer.'

'Do you mind if I walk you home tonight?' he asks, his eyes looking into mine.

'Of course.' I could think of nothing worse than going home alone to find the place empty. 'I'd like that,' I add.

'It's going to be okay,' he says, sounding so certain my own doubts waiver for a moment. He takes hold of my hand and squeezes it reassuringly. His hand is so firm and warm. It's good to know, no matter what happens, he will be here for me.

He traces his thumb along the ridge of my palm causing my hand to tingle in response. My eyes dart up to his and I quickly pull my hand away.

What is he doing?

He doesn't appear to have noticed anything's wrong, but I feel unsettled. Studying my hand, there's no visible damage on the surface except, where he so gently touched me with his thumb, it burns like fire from the contact.

I can't manage to look him in the eyes; instead I glare down at the offending hand.

'So I guess detention shouldn't go too much longer,' he says.

'Mmm.' I'm too distracted to articulate anything right now. I rub my hand against the beanbag, desperate to wipe away the tingling sensation he's scorched into my skin.

Sebastian is just a friend I tell myself. A really good friend, but he's *just* a friend. We will never be more than that.

CHAPTER TWO

Sebastian is talkative as we walk back to my quarters. I am silent for the most part, listening to him describe 'the big game' that happened on the weekend. Usually I would have been present for a basketball tournament. Instead, I was behind on my community service hours and spent the day helping in the kitchens.

I nod and add prompting questions at the appropriate points, but I'm not particularly interested. The nerves churning in my gut make it difficult to focus on anything other than Quinn. What if there's an official waiting at home with the news that Quinn is gone?

All too quickly we reach the area of the ARC where I live. My quarters are down the far end of the North Wing—or the 'forsaken corner' as I more fondly think of it. It's nearly always empty and this evening is no different. With worn-out paint in the hallways, desolate grey concrete floors, the strange smell of damp and rust, and darkened light fixtures that haven't been replaced in years, it's no surprise nobody wants to live here. But for some of us, especially orphans like Quinn and me, it's the perfect place to be left undisturbed.

We reach the turnoff to my corridor, which has to be one of the dimmest places in the whole of the ARC, and I stop dead in my tracks. Terror rushes through me and I feel heavy inside like my whole body has been cemented to the spot.

'I can't look,' I say to Sebastian. My mind assumes the worst. I don't want to look down the corridor to see an official standing there, positioned right by my door, in his crisp white blazer and white matching pants. Waiting to tell me the news I dread to hear.

'I'm sure there's no one there,' Sebastian says, as though he can see the chilling picture my mind paints. 'Do you want me to look for you?' he asks.

'No,' I shake my head, 'I can do this. I just need a second.'

Sebastian waits patiently by my side as I build up the courage to take a look. After what seems like an eternity, I finally brace myself and peek my head around the corner. The corridor is empty and a wave of relief hits me. There's no one there.

'She's okay?' I say the words with disbelief.

Sebastian gives my shoulder a reassuring squeeze. 'Looks like it,' he says gladly. He stands back and allows me to go first.

I rush down the hallway towards my room, confident now there's no one here. An official would wait all day to deliver the news your loved one was gone. It was a sign of respect but also, I suspect, a way of ensuring those left behind are compliant.

Finally, after the day from hell, I can relax.

I fumble to get my swipe card out of my pocket, clumsy in my eagerness to get in and see for myself Quinn's okay.

I open the door, beaming like an idiot, ready to give Quinn a hard time for being so worried. But my face drops and my heart plummets as the doors swings in.

The room is empty.

I STARE AT THE SPARSE, empty shell of a room hoping to see evidence Quinn's been back, but the room is just as I left it. The two small metal beds are pushed into the corners, their bright white sheets flattened over them, just as they were this morning. Quinn's treasured Vogue magazine lies open on the plain, white bedside table that stretches between our two mattresses, still opened to the same page she left it on last night, and her makeup continues its messy possession, all over the top, of the only dressing table in our small room.

As I stare into it, an overwhelming sense of detachment engulfs me and any feelings of warmth or comfort I may have felt towards this space, the only place I've ever thought of as home, disappears.

'Elle...' The echo of Sebastian's pleading voice registers on the outer edge of my awareness. I stagger into the room, all the while staring at Quinn's empty bed.

'Where is she?' is all I can manage to say; as if maybe she's hiding under the bed, or maybe she's gone to get dinner.

Sebastian comes up behind me and I sense him begin to gently rub my arms in what I suppose he assumes is a comforting way. I feel so detached from my body though I can barely feel it.

'No,' I shake my head, 'No, there's no way she's been taken.'

I instinctively bring up Quinn's username on my cuff.

'C'mon, c'mon,' I say, hitting connect. The blue light dances across the display, but eventually it winks out as the comm disconnects. Barely a second passes before I've hit connect again.

'Elle maybe you should have a seat...'

'She's not gone Sebastian. She can't be,' I mutter to myself. 'There was no official. She has to be here.'

'Elle!' Sebastian grabs a hold of my shoulders and spins me round to face him. 'I don't want her to be tainted either, but if she's not answering her comm...'

I drop my arm down as my attempted comm times out yet again and I look up at him. Sebastian's brow is furrowed with concern and his eyes are dark with anxiety.

He thinks she's gone.

'I'd *know* if she was tainted,' I say, my voice betraying my uncertainty.

'There's no way you could know...'

My eyes drop down, looking away from his pitying stare. He's right of course, but I don't want to hear it. We don't know anything about what being tainted actually means. All we know is it's an after effect from the asteroid causing people to get sick. We don't know anything about the symptoms, only they're picked up in our annual testing. There's no way I'd have been able to tell.

'She hasn't been taken Sebastian,' I say firmly, taking a step backwards out of his grasp. 'She wouldn't just leave me.'

'She wouldn't have had a choice...' His words seem to linger in the silence of the room.

I hate that word. *Choice*. It's always sounded like such a luxury, but down here there are only so many choices you get to make and whether you're taken is not one of them. Though some have tried...

'What if she went through with it?' I say, as the memory of Quinn's words this morning resurface. 'What if she tried to hide?'

My stomach does an uneasy lurch and a wave of nausea hits me. No one ever hides and gets away with it. I click connect on my cuff again, more urgently this time. My hands shake visibly. In fact, my whole body feels weak like I haven't eaten in days.

'I don't feel so good,' I say, swaying unsteadily on my feet.

Sebastian takes a hold of me and guides me towards the bed. He sits on the mattress and I drop down to sit next to him, letting my head droop against his shoulder.

'I can't lose someone else,' I whisper to him. He doesn't respond. I doubt he knows what to say. Instead he wraps his arm around me and pulls me close.

'I'm sure she's out celebrating,' he eventually says. 'You know her. She may be ditzy sometimes, but she's not stupid. She wouldn't have tried to hide.'

I don't know whether to feel better or worse about this, but he's right. She's never been one to hide from confrontation or danger. She's either out socialising or she's... I can't bear to even think the word.

'Do you remember that first day you met Quinn?' Sebastian asks.

'How can I forget?' I say with a sad laugh. It was just after April was taken. Quinn had been busy flirting with some guy who was *way* too old for her, but then she saw me walking down the hallway crying. She stopped everything to come and talk to me, to check if I was okay. She's never been one to beat around the bush.

'Do you remember what you said to her?' Sebastian asks gently.

I take a deep breath and slowly blow it out. 'That I had nothing left to lose.' The words seem to stick in my throat as I say them. I felt like I had lost everything after April was gone. All I wanted was to be found tainted and to be taken away too.

'She gave me a hug and told me it wasn't the end, and if she had anything to do with it I'd at the very least be stuck with her.' I give another sad laugh and wipe away a tear that has found its way down my cheek.

My life completely changed that day. After April was taken I'd been determined to never get close to anyone ever again, but Quinn's personality was infectious. It wasn't long before she'd added herself to the small list of people I consider my family.

Sebastian peers down at me and smiles. 'She certainly came through in that respect.' The smile drops from his face as he continues. 'I know you still like to think you're that girl who has no one left, but you're wrong. You have so many friends, Dad still sees you like a daughter and you have me. You're not alone anymore. You never really have been.'

I lift my head off Sebastian's shoulder and turn to him. For such a long time I've felt like it's just me against the world and I have nobody to lean on. Over the years I've become better at masking it. How did he know I still felt that way?

After several moments, I look away, uncomfortable with the concern I see in his eyes. I hate that he can see straight through the walls I put up. 'I can't just sit here and wait any longer,' I say. 'I need to go to the hospital. I need to do *something*.'

He exhales loudly, as though disappointed with my response. 'We both know that's a bad idea, you'll get in trouble,' he says.

'So?' I respond, unemotionally.

'So, they don't want you asking questions.'

'I don't care what they want!'

As soon as the words have left my mouth I gasp and clamp my hand across my lips. I shouldn't have said it, even if we are in the privacy of my room.

Sebastian falls silent and looks around the room warily, as if worried the walls have ears.

'I ... I didn't mean it. You know I didn't—'

A loud banging at the door causes me to halt. How could they know what I said?

I quickly realise it's highly unlikely I was overheard. No, whoever stands on the other side of the door isn't here for me.

I slip Sebastian's arm from around my shoulders and go to stand, my legs trembling beneath me. For a moment I stare at the door and listen to the loud thuds that cause the frame to shudder.

I turn back to Sebastian. My fear must be clearly painted across my face because he quickly stands.

'Let me get it,' he insists, standing to face the door.

I take a hesitant step backwards, my arms hugged tightly around my body.

This is it. The moment I've been dreading all day has finally arrived.

CHAPTER THREE

The banging at the door becomes louder and more incessant. Sebastian gives me a grim nod, as he clasps his hand around the door handle and slowly pulls it back.

I hold my breath as it opens.

'Quinn?' I breathe, as the door opens fully to reveal her standing in the entrance.

'Geez Sebastian, took you long enough!' Quinn says, as she enters, looking as though nothing has happened.

'Quinn!' I exclaim, running forward and grabbing her up in a hug. 'I was so worried.'

She merely laughs in response. 'Elle, chill! I'm fine, you're fine, we're all just fine.' She laughs again. 'Actually, I'm more than fine. I'm ecstatic! Just been on a date with a super cute doctor from the Hospital Wing.'

Sebastian steps towards Quinn. 'So you let Elle worry all this time you might have been taken, while you go on a date? Don't you care what she went through?' An incredulous tone creeps into his voice.

'Calm down tiger,' Quinn chides.

'Why didn't you answer her comms?' he persists.

'I was busy,' she says with a shrug, walking past us both to sit on her bed. She picks up her Vogue magazine from the bedside table and absently gazes at the amalgamation of faces that dot the cover of the 150th anniversary edition. There's usually a reverence, bordering on obsession, in the way she looks at that thing, but tonight she seems disinterested. She leans herself back against the pillow, with her most prized possession from the past, and begins to carefully flick through it.

Her casual approach to the whole thing seems to really get on Sebastian's nerves. I can see his face gearing up for a confrontation, so I walk over to him and touch his arm. I ever so slightly shake my head and mouth 'don't'. He nods back at me, but I can tell by the look in his eyes and his tight set jaw, he's still angry.

'It's getting late. Maybe it's time for you to go,' I tell Sebastian. My voice is calm, but my eyes tell a different story. 'Don't start something,' they warn.

'Yeah, okay,' he responds. 'Bye Quinn.' He stresses each word slowly and harshly.

'Bye Sebastian,' she mimics back to him, not bothering to look up from her magazine.

Sebastian's face transforms as he looks at me. He gives me his easy, warm smile that has been known to devastate other girls. Me? I'm unaffected. *Totally* unaffected.

'I'll see you tomorrow,' he says, grabbing his bag and slinging it over his shoulder. He turns to leave, but before he goes I call his name, causing him to pause by the door and turn back to me.

'Thanks ... for everything tonight,' I say, my words garbling in their rush to get out.

His lips curve into a pleased smile. 'It was no problem.' His eyes fall from mine to stare at the floor. He almost looks embarrassed, but I can't for the life of me figure out why. Without another word he quickly leaves.

As soon as the door shuts Quinn drops her magazine back on top of the bedside table. 'Finally! I thought he'd never leave!' she complains.

When I turn back to her, I find her face transformed. The carefree look that had moments ago graced her face is gone.

'What's wrong?'

'Noth—'

'Quinn, I know that face. What's wrong?'

She pulls herself to the edge of the bed and dangles her legs down over the side.

'You're probably going to think I'm crazy, well, crazier than normal. But people have been talking,' she says quietly. 'There hasn't been anyone taken in over six months...'

'So? That's a good thing right?'

She shakes her head. 'I'm not so sure. I've been hearing lots of people are about to be taken. I'd dismissed it as idle ARC gossip, but today my testing felt off, like something was different. It was almost as though they wanted my result to come back tainted.'

She bends her head over to look down at her hands fidgeting in her lap. 'I don't know. The whole thing just has me worried. I have a feeling something bad is going to happen...'

'There's nothing for you to worry about. You aren't tainted. You won't have to worry for another year,' I say, in an attempt to cheer her up.

'You're right. I'm being silly.' She laughs lightly at herself, but the sound is stilted and there's a tension across her forehead. She's visibly still upset.

'So, wanna hear about my date with Dr. Delicious?' she asks, wiggling her eyebrows at me.

I laugh and go sit at the end of her bed. I'm so happy she's okay I'd be willing to hear her talk about anything. As she talks enthusiastically about the date though, I find myself focusing more on what she said before. For something to unnerve Quinn like that, and affect her usual chirpy self for even a second, it must be serious.

The next morning I wake abruptly, as Quinn flicks on the overhead light. I groan and throw my sheet over my face. Moments later her hairdryer is fired up and I groan even louder. I know I must be over the concern I felt for her yesterday because, so far today, I think I'm going to kill her.

The high-pitched whine of the hairdryer rackets loudly from the other side of the sheet. There's no way I can sleep under these conditions so I restlessly shove my sheet off and down the bed, then prop myself up against the wall. Rubbing my eyes, I wait for them to adjust to the light.

Quinn is already dressed in her greys for the day. She's one of the few people in the ARC who look good in the regulation clothes we are required to wear. I check the time on my cuff. Six in the morning —*you've got to be kidding me.*

'Why are you up so early?' I grumble. Quinn spins around and turns off the dryer.

'Oh sorry Elle! I didn't mean to wake you. I have the early shift this morning.' Her voice is energetic and she's way too animated for this hour. Especially considering she kept me awake for half the night talking about her date.

Quinn graduated from school three years ago and now works in 'data and admin' for the hospital. The amount of effort she puts in to getting ready for a day at work, in some small forgotten shoebox of a room, always amazes me.

Like she needs to put in any effort. Her long blonde hair always manages to fall in perfect large, soft curls and she has a face that probably belongs on the cover of her old Vogue magazine. Like mine, her pale skin shines as a signature of a life lived underground, but her golden hair and bright green eyes are so much more exciting than my own brown hair, blue-eyed combo.

'I promise I'll be quick!' she pleads. I merely groan again in response and lean my head against the wall. She rushes around the room throwing items in her bag and checks herself in the mirror one last time, before walking to the door. She places her hand against the light switch as she goes to leave.

'On or off?'

'Off! Off!' I beg.

'Okay!' She laughs as she turns the light off.

'Have a good day,' I mumble sleepily, as the door slams shut and the hard, wooden doorframe shudders.

I settle back down into bed. After several minutes of tossing, turning and rearranging I can tell I'm too restless to get back to sleep. I lie with my eyes open, wide-awake.

Even with the light off there is no true darkness in the ARC. Deep blue sensor lights line the point where all walls meet the floor and a small night-light illuminates the door handle. *What I'd give for complete darkness right now.*

I keep trying to get comfortable, but it's pointless. I'm awake and there's no chance of sleep now. Reluctant to leave the bed's warmth, but unable to lie restlessly any longer, I get up, grab my towel and head for the communal showers down the hallway.

The hot steamy water feels amazing, but for some reason I can't relax. I feel fidgety and agitated, like bugs are squirming under my skin, making it hard for me to stand still. I should be relieved knowing Quinn's okay. Instead I feel completely on edge. I keep replaying what she said last night over and over in my mind. Surely they didn't want her to be tainted?

I'm still restless when I get back to the room, and having to tear through my drawers to try and find a clean set of greys doesn't seem to be making me any calmer.

As I begin to brush a comb through my hair, my eyes fall down to the corner of a notebook that peeks out from under Quinn's bed. Curious, I bend down to pick it up. The book is larger than I'd expected and has 'Sebastian Scott' written across the cover, in his heavy, messy scrawl.

I have seen him with the thing countless times; it's always tucked up under his arm, almost an extension of himself. On the rare occasions I see him draw, he will prop the book at such an angle to keep his work hidden. He's never shared the book's contents with me though, and I have to admit I'm curious.

The book feels like fire in my fingers and, despite my temptation to open it and see what's inside, I know its pages hold something deeply personal for Sebastian. I couldn't open this book anymore than I could read his diary.

I drop the book onto to my bed, intending to keep it there until I leave for school. It lands at an awkward angle though and falls open to reveal one of its pages. I find myself unable to look away and am captivated by the pictures that cover the paper.

It's not just one drawing, but many that fit in any and every spare space on the page. From afar the page is awash with charcoal, but looking closely I can depict each object. There are places like the Atrium and the library, but also drawings of things he couldn't possibly remember, like the sun and the stars. They're beautiful and so intricately drawn and interwoven between each other that anyone would admire his talent.

I freeze when my eyes find their way to one particular sketch. There, drawn on the page, is a perfect likeness of me. I grab the book up to look at it more closely. The drawing is so detailed and it looks as though it must've taken him hours to do. He's even managed to capture the small chickenpox scar on my chin. I touch the spot, almost as if to check I haven't imagined it.

Looking at the page, I start to feel uncomfortable. Why did he draw this? I quickly slam the notebook shut. I really ought to get this back to him.

CHAPTER FOUR

After a minute of knocking on the door to Sebastian's quarters, he finally opens it. He's rubbing his eyes and yawning as he stands in the doorway. He's topless and his pyjama pants hang loosely off of his waist. I stand there speechless and can literally feel my jaw drop. His arms and chest have filled out, and his stomach is flat and firm. *Since when has Sebastian gotten so grown up?*

His eyes, still glazed over with sleep, look down at me and he gives me a drowsy half smile in greeting. 'Morning,' he yawns.

I realise I'm still staring at him and quickly look away, feeling slightly flustered. Nothing more awkward than being caught eyeing up your best friend.

'Sorry about the early call but,' I hold out his sketchbook, 'I think this dropped out of your bag last night and wanted to make sure it got back to you.'

He seems uncomfortable as he takes it from me, and a flash of worry seems to flicker in his eyes. It's gone quickly though, replaced by his usual confidence. 'Thanks. Do you want to come in?' he asks.

My eyes dart nervously away from his as I hesitate.

'Dad's not here,' he says, guessing at my thoughts.

My body relaxes and as it does a pang of guilt tugs inside me. I hate I'm relieved he's not here. It's not that I don't want to see Adam. It's just he's so sad and quiet these days. It's horrible to see him that way, especially when I know I'm one of the reasons behind it.

'Well, I did bring breakfast,' I say, nodding down to the container of porridge I hold with a mug of tea cradled precariously on top.

Sebastian's stomach growls in response and he laughs, taking the container from me as I follow him inside. The quarters are simple, like most residences in the ARC, but Sebastian and Adam have certainly managed to make it distinctively their own with small touches here and there that I love.

A tattered football poster hangs from the wall next to Adam's engineering degree and obviously loved books sit in piles atop one of the dressers. The backs of their spines are thoroughly crinkled from years of reading. Then across the room, sitting on the bedside table, my favourite item: a tarnished silver picture frame with a photo of Sebastian's parents on their wedding day.

I walk over to the picture and gently pick it up to look at his mum and dad. They seem so carefree and happy in the unnaturally green garden under the bright, blue cloudless sky. In the bushes behind them pink roses burst out at random matching Adam's perfectly adorned tie and corsage. The only thing remotely similar to anything down here is the pure white of Isabel's long flowing wedding dress that matches the pale walls that surround me. Sebastian's dad is barely recognisable in the picture. He now carries the deep-set frown across his forehead that so many adults in this place seem to wear.

As I set the picture frame down, my eyes are drawn to Sebastian's unkempt bed. An assortment of grey clothing is strewn across it and spills onto the floor—Sebastian's of course. My fingers almost itch with the need to clean the clothes up.

He lives alone here with his Dad. They moved into smaller quarters after I moved in with Quinn. I always feel a sense of sadness when I come here. It reminds me of the gaping hole left in our lives. How unfair that both his mum and sister were taken. I'd like to think at least Sebastian is lucky he still has one family member left, but the way Adam has become completely withdrawn, I sometimes wonder if he feels like he's alone.

I take a seat at the small metal table that sits in the centre of the room. Sebastian throws a top on and then joins me. Sitting in the chair opposite, he clears his throat. 'So what was the deal with Quinn last night?'

'You know what she's like,' I mumble.

'Yeah, but I guess I just expected her to be more considerate.' He pauses to open the porridge container, which cracks loudly as he pulls off the lid. Looking up at me, he scratches the stubble across his jaw as though confused. 'She could have at least answered your comm.'

'Her heart is in the right place,' I respond. 'I'm just glad she's okay.'

He shrugs like he's not too fussed, but I know it's just for show. They may have a love-hate relationship, but he's always respected her for the way she's looked after me.

'So what's with the early morning wake up call? Did you miss me?' he jokes.

'Oh yeah, couldn't spend another second without you,' I say, my voice thick with sarcasm.

'Thought so.' He attempts to cover a smile, and offers the first spoonful of porridge out to me, but I shake my head and refuse. I've never had much of a stomach for the stuff and unfortunately it's all they usually serve at breakfast.

'It may have been Quinn needing an early start,' I explain.

'Of course,' he says, through a mouth full of food.

I ignore his judgemental tone and take a sip of my precious tea, relishing the feeling as the warm liquid slides down my throat. It's been such a long time since I've had enough points for one, and it tastes even better than I remember. After another sip I place the mug down on the table and allow my fingers to faintly trace the lip of the cup. 'Quinn said something strange to me last night.'

Sebastian looks up from his food. 'Which was?'

My fingers stop their tracing as I think of how to put it. 'She seemed to think lots of people are about to be taken. That they actually *want* people to be tainted and acted like it during her testing.'

Sebastian's face doesn't change and I wonder for a second if he's even heard me. I wrap my hands around my mug and bring it to my lips again. 'I don't know, it's crazy.' I take a deep mouthful of tea and look away from him, regretting having raised the subject at all.

'I've heard similar things,' Sebastian eventually says. 'But I never thought it was true.'

His words are thoughtful and I get the impression he's spent some time considering the rumours. I look back to find him staring at me. 'What do you think now?' I ask.

He sighs and places his spoon down on the table. 'I think I'm sick of all the secrets in this place.'

'That's hardly something new...' I venture, uncertainty clawing at my insides. He's acting so serious and I worry what he's thinking.

'No. It's not.'

The room falls quiet. The silence is filled with tension and the atmosphere heavy with words unsaid. I clasp my tea closer to me and take several long drinks of it to fill the void left by the lack of conversation. We've always been so easy around each other, but I don't know how to deal with him when he acts like this.

'Ahh!' I jump up quickly. Somehow I've completely missed my mouth and poured hot tea down my top. I try to hold the material away from my body so it doesn't continue to scold me.

'Shit,' Sebastian swears under his breath as he jumps up and throws me a towel. I catch it and try to dab the wet top dry, but it's soaked and from the looks of things it's also stained.

'It could be worse. At least the tea had cooled off a bit,' I say. 'I'm just sad I didn't get to finish it.'

Sebastian walks over to his drawers. Bending down he pulls out a regulation grey top and passes it to me. 'Here. It's going to be too big for you, but at least you won't be wet.'

'Thanks.' I clutch the top awkwardly in my arms, waiting for him to look away. 'Where should I...'

'Oh,' Sebastian flushes and hastily turns around. 'I promise I won't peek.'

I can feel my cheeks redden in response, and try to laugh it off. 'Sure you won't,' I joke, hoping he doesn't, but also uncertain how I'd feel if he did.

As I lift my top off to replace it with his I glance over my shoulder. Sebastian stands determinedly facing the opposite wall with his hands over his eyes. I smile to myself and quickly pop his top over my head.

It's massive and the sleeves hang to my knees. I guess it was to be expected considering how much larger Sebastian is. 'So what do you think?' I ask seriously.

Sebastian turns back to me and bursts out laughing. His laughter almost makes being scorched by my drink worth it. At least he's snapped out of his mood.

'I think we're going to need to roll those sleeves up!' he says, walking over to come and help me.

He stops right in front of me, gently holds up my hand and starts rolling the ridiculous sleeves. I take in a deep breath, trying to ignore how uncomfortable I feel at his proximity, but he stands so close that as I breathe in I can't ignore how good he smells.

'All done,' he says quietly, his voice is rough and he clears his throat as though uncomfortable with the sound. His hand still holds mine and he begins softly tracing his thumb over the back of it, just like he'd done in the library.

'Uh—thanks.' I pull my hand from his and take a quick step back. I can't let him get close like that again. Confusion touches his eyes and he seems upset by my reaction.

'That's done the trick,' I mutter, frowning. I don't know what's gotten into him or me. He's never acted this way before and I've never been so jumpy around him. 'I should go,' I continue.

I start to walk towards the door, but as I reach my hand towards the door handle I turn and say, 'I'll catch you at school.' It's said as light heartedly as I can muster, like everything's normal, but he merely shrugs in response.

As the door bangs shut behind me, I am overwhelmed by the feeling I've done something wrong, but that's not what worries me the most. It's the feeling something has changed between Sebastian and me—and I'm not sure if it's a good thing.

CHAPTER FIVE

'Wake up Elle!' Gemma calls at me. I look over in response and realise she's just thrown me the basketball and it's sailed straight over my head.

'You could at least *try* to help us win!' she jokes, as I run to retrieve the ball.

I can't blame her for being frustrated by my lack of enthusiasm for the game today. I've been seriously distracted all day by Sebastian's absence from school.

Not once did I see him today, and I *always* manage to bump into him, or at the very least see him during breaks. Even tonight, when school finally finished for the day, I would've expected him to turn up for a game. Maybe he's avoiding me?

'Are you throwing that ball back anytime soon?' Gemma yells. I still hold it absently in my hands.

'Oh, right.' I snap out of my troubling thoughts and throw the ball back to her.

'You're fighting a losing battle there Gems,' Cam, one of the boys on the other team jests. 'If you want to win you should come and join the better side.'

'What can I say, I just love an underdog,' she retorts. He raises his eyebrows in response, takes two long strides over to her and hoists her over his shoulder.

'Put me down Cam!' she squeals with laughter.

The game is pretty much over after this as the two of them chase each other up and down the court flirting. The rest of us retreat to the side of the court.

'I don't think you're the underdog,' Jase, one of the boys from the other team, says to me.

'Thanks Jase, but I really was playing pretty atrocious tonight,' I respond.

'True,' he laughs. 'Hopefully you'll be better next week.'

'God I hope so!' I take a seat on the ground next to Amy.

'I'm surprised you came out tonight,' I say to Amy, as I ease myself onto the polished wooden floor. She never plays sport unless it's during school hours, choosing to use most of her time studying. I practically never spend any time with her outside class.

She looks out across the court, her eyes almost sad as she smooths down her long, black ponytail. 'My parents are insisting I immerse myself in *all* aspects of my education.'

I wrinkle my face up at the thought. It must suck having to constantly live up to parents' expectations. I can't imagine Amy ever being a disappointment though.

'You're pretty good you know. You definitely have the height for basketball,' I say.

'Just a shame about my two left feet,' she grumbles. 'Speaking of left feet. You coming to the dance?'

'Yeah. When is it again?' I've completely forgotten about it with the stress of Quinn's testing.

'A few weeks time. It should be good!'

'Mmm,' I agree. The school hosts a dance for all the high school students a few times a year, but I'm not really into the dancing bit so much. I do like the outfits we're allowed to wear though.

Usually straight after school on a Friday everyone heads to the costume room, where donated clothes from before impact are held. Each student is allowed to rent one outfit to wear to the dance instead of our greys. While the ARC doesn't have enough outfits from before impact to use for everyday wear, the school does have enough available for special occasions.

'I just hope I'm lucky enough to get a good dress for it,' I say. So many of the clothes have fallen into disrepair, it can be a struggle to find something half decent.

Amy nods eagerly in response. 'Yeah, I probably wouldn't go if I ended up with something bad. Some of the girls can be so mean.'

She doesn't need to elaborate, I already know exactly who she's talking about: Kate Evans. I'm pretty certain she made two girls and a teacher cry at our last dance. That girl knows how to create trouble and, with her dad on the Council, she's not afraid of anyone.

Amy checks the time on her cuff. 'It's getting pretty late. I'm meant to meet my parents for dinner, and I really need to get started on that English assignment.'

'I thought it wasn't due until next week?'

'It's not,' she shrugs.

'You're such a nerd,' I laugh. 'I should probably head off as well.' I turn to the court and see Gemma and Cam have stopped chasing each other. Instead she stands there with her eyes riveted to him, her fingers twisting unconsciously through the ends of her hair. She looks completely infatuated, and he looks like he has it just as bad.

'Gemma!' I call out. 'I'm going! You coming?'

She looks back and forth, torn between Cam and me. I try not to appear too pleased by the situation. It's nice to see him finally making a move.

'You know what?' I continue. 'I've got some homework I need to do, I'll just catch you in class tomorrow.'

'Okay, see you in the morning,' she responds happily, unable to keep the excitement from her voice. We wave goodbye to each other and I follow Amy out.

'What's the deal with Cam and Gemma?' she asks curiously.

'I've got no idea. They've been flirting with each other for a while now. I guess I'll be hearing all about it tomorrow though.'

Amy chuckles in response. 'Yeah I imagine you would.'

After walking through several long, almost identical corridors we reach the Atrium, the point in which all wings of the ARC converge. I stand and admire the huge, bright hall that reaches up all the way to the ceiling of the ARC, several hundred meters above. Huge television screens line the walls and long glass-floored walkways that connect the wings for each level are suspended above.

Masses of people rhythmically flow across the walkways above. I squint my eyes to see if I can count how many are walking on the top walkway, but there's no one up there today. Even stories below, the tiny figures are hard to make out.

The top levels have always intrigued me. Regardless of which wing you're in you can't seem to access them. When we were younger, April, Sebastian and I spent a day climbing up many flights of stairs in each wing attempting to reach the top. But no matter how hard we tried we always ended up two floors below the ceiling.

Some man bumps into me. 'Sorry,' he says, walking on. I turn to respond but he's already disappeared. As usual the Atrium is hectic.

Amy points her thumb towards the West Wing entrance. 'This is me.'

'Oh, I'm heading over there.' I wave my hand in the direction of the North Wing. 'You'll have to come out to basketball again soon.'

'Yeah, maybe,' she responds, looking unconvinced. She takes just a few steps away and is quickly lost in the crowd. As I veer towards the North Wing one of the screens catches my eye. I walk closer to it. Most just show feed from the surface, but no one is interested in viewing the boring, desolate wasteland above.

As I near one screen I recognise the vast snow-blown landscape with its expanse of frosty cracks that quake across the ground. Dotted across the horizon are lone, charred and blackened trees and overhead clouds gather, dark and violent with ugly tinges of purple Lysart that constantly reminds us of the asteroid that doomed us all. They thunder across the empty wastes wreaking havoc on the deadened earth. So thick and heavy with sediment, tossed up into the atmosphere after impact, they never stop for breath, always smothering the earth far below. The surface. My uninterested eyes skim past the screen and on to the next one, which shows the ARC news.

A woman sits in a smart black suit, in front of a soft blue background. Using a very serious tone of voice she announces, 'A man was arrested today after attempting to break into his neighbour's quarters.' The screen flicks to CCTV footage of the man being arrested by officials. They are brutal as they shove him up against the wall. After several attempts to force himself free the man's body slowly sags as he is sedated.

The screen flicks back to the news reporter. 'He is currently being held by officials and will face a hearing before the Council in the morning.' She pauses before she continues. 'In other news, citizens are reminded that upon any symptoms of a fever they are to report immediately to the Hospital Wing. Symptoms include...'

I ignore the television as the broadcast breaks back into regular reminders. What kind of idiot would try to break into someone's quarters?

'Elle?' I hear Sebastian's voice behind me. I turn to see him watching the screen from over my shoulder. 'I was just coming to look for you,' he says, half distracted by the news.

My hand drifts up to clasp at my necklace as I watch him awkwardly. I have no idea what to say to him. Has he been avoiding me all day or am I reading into his disappearance from school too much?

He frowns at the screen before focusing down on my face. 'There's something I want to show you. Would you come check it out with me?'

I hesitate in my response. I don't like agreeing to things when I don't know what I'm getting myself into. It's Sebastian though, so I trust him. I've barely begun to nod when he grabs my hand and starts guiding me towards the West Wing. 'We have to be quick.'

I stumble over my feet as I attempt to keep up with him. He doesn't seem upset at all about this morning. It's like it never happened.

'Where are we going?' I ask, as we weave our way between the throng of people.

'You'll see...' is all he says as he leads me under the large pillared archway and up the extravagant marbled staircase that marks the entrance to the West Wing.

I suppress a groan as we enter. I'd probably prefer to be kicked out onto the surface than to visit the West Wing. The whole place is so pretentious, not to mention a complete maze. I always manage to get lost on the rare occasions I find my way over here.

The obvious wealth in the area has always succeeded in making me feel unwelcome. All the people who were considered important enough to get an invitation to bunker down in the ARC when the asteroid hit live here. Nowadays I have no idea what most of them were once famed for, but they all still act like they're above everyone who lives in the North Wing.

Sebastian gives my hand a reassuring squeeze and turns back to look at me with his cheeky smile. 'Stop stressing. I'll have you back to your beloved North Wing in no time.'

I glare at him and then look away, refusing to meet his gaze. I hear him chuckle as he tugs me into a faster pace.

We walk for a while down several corridors, each just as lavish as the next. Large slabs of white marble tiles cover the floor and the doors are all made from frosted glass. Elaborate chandeliers hang from the ceilings of popular intersections and once priceless paintings are hung in special, protective glass boxes that line the walls of most walkways.

Sebastian comes to a sudden halt and I in turn slam into his back. 'We're here,' he states, simply.

'Where's here?' I ask, edging my way around him to take a look. I fail to see anything special about where he's brought me. The corridor is very much the same as every other in the wing.

Sebastian points to the door closest to us. 'Do you know where that leads?' he asks.

I shake my head and take a closer look at the door. It's just like the other frosted glass doors in the wing, however, as I look more carefully I notice the biometric security lock that protects it. My stomach drops and begins to feel empty. There are only a handful of places in the ARC with so much security on them. I've never been into one and I'm fairly certain I never want to.

'What's in there Sebastian?' I ask him, already dreading the answer.

He's already taken a step towards the door and is looking at it the way a kid's eyes devour the sight of an unopened Christmas present.

'You'll have to wait and see,' he says, secretively. 'I'll give you a hint though, the ARC blueprints I've been studying for my engineering apprenticeship say it's restricted...'

'Restricted?' I repeat. This is *so* not a good idea. 'How would we even get in there?' I say, eyeing up the security.

He wriggles his fingers in front of my face. 'Some of us have contacts.'

I reach out and touch Sebastian's arm, stopping him from moving any closer to the door. 'This is a bad idea and you know it. We shouldn't be messing around with a restricted zone,' I warn.

He turns back to look at me. 'Aren't you sick of all their lies?' he asks. 'Don't you want to finally get some answers? I thought you of all people would understand.'

'I do understand, but it's *restricted* Sebastian. It's too dangerous. No answers are worth this.'

Sebastian struggles to hide his disappointment with what I've said. 'I didn't ask you here to try and get you into trouble. I thought you would want to come. You've always been up for bending a few rules.'

'Hardly,' I scoff. 'I think we both know it's been a long time since I've done anything that would get me more than a few extra community service hours, worst-case scenario. Going into a biometrically secured room is *bad.* You don't even know if anyone's in there.'

Sebastian considers my face before he continues, 'Elle, I don't want you doing something you're not comfortable with. You don't have to come with me.'

Before I can answer he turns and boldly walks towards the door. I want to delay, to consider the options before committing to such an idiotic act, but I already know I won't let him go in there alone. *Damn him.*

With not even half his courage, I follow. There's no way in hell this is going to end well.

CHAPTER SIX

'You're going to get us in so much trouble,' I tell Sebastian, as I step closer to the door. Every fibre in my being is tense and I know, beyond a shadow of a doubt, this is a bad idea. Sebastian's plan, or lack thereof, is certifiably crazy.

It's clear he's only doing this after hearing the rumours I repeated to him last night. He's always been slightly obsessed with conspiracy theories about the tainted; I guess it's only natural considering the family he's lost because of it. I should try to stop him, but the closer we edge towards the door, the less inclined I feel to turn back.

Curiosity begins to prickle just beneath my skin, and I wonder if we really could uncover some of the mysteries that have always troubled us. Maybe I should be committed to the loony ward too?

Sebastian's courage seems to waiver for a moment when he gets to the door. He stands there with his hand reached out, frozen still in the air. It hovers for a few seconds, but then his resolve strengthens and he places it down on the scanner.

We both hold our breath as we wait to see if his fingerprints will be accepted. The scanner beeps though and there's the distinctive sound of a lock unbolting.

'If I ever find out who helps you with this crap, I swear I'm going to kill them,' I mutter under my breath, as the door swings inwards, not caring whether Sebastian hears me or not.

I don't know what I expected, but a small, bare chamber with one lone couch and another door on the wall opposite is not it. I almost laugh with relief. All that security was for nothing.

'Okay, satisfied?' I ask. 'There's nothing in here.'

Sebastian ignores me and continues across the room, heading for the door on the opposite wall. He quickly disappears inside it and I rush to follow him, afraid to be left behind in the empty chamber.

Taking a deep breath in, I approach the door and slowly push it open. My breath catches in my throat though when I see the room on the other side.

'What is this place?' I wonder aloud, as I walk inside.

A long mahogany table stretches down the centre of the room surrounded by huge leather chairs the colour of dirt and rust. An unused fireplace, flanked by two well-lit niches, is located on the far wall. Inside the niches are the busts of two men—most likely old, long dead presidents from before impact.

Though the focus of the room is on the table, my eyes are drawn to the plush carpet, with its striking shades of sapphire and gold intricately woven into a fern like pattern. Nowhere else in the ARC has carpet and it somehow seems to make the room even more intimidating.

'It's the Council Chambers,' Sebastian responds, calmly.

My head whips around to look at him. 'The Council Chambers?' I repeat the words in disbelief.

They've always been nothing more than another room in the ARC I never expected to see; one cloaked in so many layers of secrecy and mystery I almost began to doubt it even existed. As I look around at the sumptuous furnishings of the room I can't deny the place does indeed exist.

'We *so* shouldn't be in here,' I whisper, my voice barely audible, even to my own ears. 'We should get out of here,' I add, looking back towards the door.

'You worry too much,' Sebastian says, taking a seat in one of the large leather chairs. He props his feet up on the table, looking very much at ease. 'When will we ever get another chance like this?'

Never—especially not if we're caught in here. I try not to think of the consequences of being discovered, but they plague the forefront of my mind. In my nervous state, an eternity of community service, imprisonment and death by exposure all seem like highly possible, rational options if we're caught. Maybe death by exposure is reaching a little far. I've never actually heard of anyone being sent to the surface to die so I suspect that one is more of a myth. Well, I hope.

I glance back towards the door. Someone could come in at any moment and we've already been in here too long. When I turn around Sebastian has left his chair and gone to open the only other door in the room.

'What are you doing?' I race after him as he disappears inside only to find the door does not lead to another room, but a closet.

'Now, tell me seriously, what do you think?' Sebastian emerges from the closet in one of the gowns only those on the Council wear. He runs his hand through his messy, brown hair and looks down at the long, black robe.

'I think you're going to get us in a whole lot of trouble if you don't stop playing dress-up and leave with me.' I turn to look at the door again. We should really get out of here.

His face drops. 'Ah you're no fun. Where's the adventurous Elle gone?'

'Unfortunately "adventure Elle" prefers not to cross that silly line when adventure becomes danger,' I respond. 'Please Sebastian. You're being careless and all you seem to be doing in here is messing around. Can we just go already?'

He opens his mouth to respond, but shuts it quickly as we hear the sound of several deep male voices coming from the chamber we'd entered through.

'Quick, get in here.' He grabs my hand and pulls me towards the closet.

'I ... I can't,' I stutter, as I look at the small, packed room.

Sebastian stops and turns to me, taking hold of my other hand. 'I will be with you the whole time. I won't let you go for a second. You can do this.'

I try not to think about what we're about to do and simply nod, allowing Sebastian to guide me inside the closet. He shuts the door behind us, encasing the small room in darkness with only the smallest crack of light streaming in from under the door.

The space is cramped and warm, and with all the Council cloaks rammed in here it's suffocatingly small. I take a deep breath in and slowly blow it out, trying to ignore the way my stomach has dropped and how my lungs appear to have shrunk.

Sebastian pulls me to the back of the closet so we are masked behind the gowns. The air is stale and thick with dust, which makes it more difficult to breathe.

'It's really small in here...' I moan quietly to Sebastian.

'It's okay. You're going to be okay.' He helps me to sit down on the floor with him and squeezes my hand. 'Just close your eyes and focus on your breathing. Imagine we're somewhere open, like the plantation. I'm sure those men aren't even on the Council. They won't be coming in here.'

I give him a small nod, though I doubt he can see it in the darkened closet, and take several deep breaths. Small beads of sweat begin to form on the back of my neck and I can feel my hands getting clammy.

Shutting my eyes, I try to imagine I'm somewhere else—anywhere else. It's not just the claustrophobic closet that has me worried though. It's the fear we might be about to get caught. Instead, I focus on the feeling of Sebastian's hand in mine. It's a small thing, a simple thing to focus on, but the feeling of our hands bound together makes me feel like I'm home. The pressure on my chest begins to lessen and my frantic heartbeat starts to slow.

It quickens again, and Sebastian's grip on my hand tightens, when we hear men entering the Council Chambers. Several are talking all at once and it's difficult to discern any individual voice.

'Are you okay?' Sebastian whispers. His breath is warm against my ear and I shiver in response.

'I'm alright,' I concede, though it's nowhere near the truth. I'm far from alright. I almost want to face the wrath of the Council just to get out of this closet. But I can't handle the idea of getting Sebastian in trouble too, even if it's his fault we're here.

A man clears his voice loudly from the other side of the door and I can hear the other men being called to order. The muffled conversations die down and one lone voice remains.

'Good evening, I would like to welcome you to this May sixteenth, 2065 emergency meeting of the ARC Council. I would like to remind you this is a closed meeting and neither the agenda nor the minutes will be published over the intranet. We're going to begin today's proceedings by hearing from Councillor Ahmed. Councillor...'

'Yes, thank you Chairman,' Ahmed begins. 'As some of you may know, this meeting has been called to deal with the fluctuations in footage of the surface. At twenty-three hundred hours last night, there was an anomaly on the footage projected to the ARC screens. It was several minutes before the anomaly was spotted by one of our technicians and in this time the footage was seen by several citizens.'

'How many?' a deep voice asks.

'It was only a handful. Most weren't watching the screens or were unsure of what they saw. There was only one who caused any difficulty.'

'Has any action been taken against this person?' the Chairman asks.

There is silence before Councillor Ahmed speaks again. 'We've made a public broadcast showing him being arrested for stealing from his neighbours. He'll be sentenced in the morning and shouldn't cause anymore trouble.'

There is silence again and as I rerun the words through my mind I realise the man I saw on the news tonight was framed. I involuntarily shudder and draw my knees up to my chest. They're acting like it was nothing.

'What are you doing about the live feed?' asks a mature woman's voice.

'I've got a team who are altering the system. The broadcast to the ARC now has a time delay of several minutes. We have set up several batches of pre-recorded footage to show should the problem arise again.'

'Ahmed, what exactly was it people saw yesterday?' says another voice.

'We're still trying to figure that out ourselves, but from what we can gather the storms that rage on the surface subsided for a few hours. The sky cleared and, it seems, there were stars.'

I inhale sharply and Sebastian clamps his hand down over my mouth.

Stars.

The dust cloud that covers the earth has always been so thick, and the storms so violent, it was hopeless to even dream that we would see them again, at least not in the foreseeable future. The sediment that clouds the air isn't supposed to settle for at least another ten years, or so we've been told.

'What does this mean?' I whisper to Sebastian.

'I wish I knew,' he whispers back.

CHAPTER SEVEN

The Council meeting continues on for the better part of an hour. There is no more talk of stars and I wonder at how the councilmen could have such an indifferent response to the discovery. The only conclusion I can come to is they were already well aware of the change in the surface conditions.

I don't know whether this is good or not.

My stomach begins to grumble in sad complaint as the time gets later. We should've had dinner ages ago and after playing basketball I'm like a fuel tank running on empty. It certainly doesn't help when one of the agenda items discussed by the Council is food rationing—like we need more restrictions on the meagre portions we already get.

I know that the meeting is finally drawing to a close when a councilman named Perkins is told his problems with the plantation irrigation system will be put on the agenda for the next meeting.

By the time the councilmen finally leave, my head is drooping down on Sebastian's shoulder and my eyes feel heavy from being in the warm, dark cupboard for such a long time.

Sebastian gently pushes the strands of hair that have fallen in front of my face back behind my ear. 'Are you awake?' he whispers.

My eyes have adjusted to the darkness in the closet now and as I yawn and glance up at him I catch a strange look in his eyes. My heart seems to stutter for a second and I almost forget he asked me a question.

'Just,' I answer, quickly looking away. I sit up straight, putting distance between us, and stretch my arms out above my head. 'Do you think it's safe to leave?'

'Only one way to find out,' he responds.

I hear him shuffle as he makes his way to the door, through the curtain of robes we hide behind. There's a soft squeak as he turns the door handle and a shaft of bright light enters as he opens the door.

'All clear,' he calls, pushing the door wide. I clamber on my knees towards the light and let out a huge sigh of relief when I'm back in the Council Chambers. Sebastian takes my hand and helps pull me off the floor. My legs feel like jelly under me after sitting still for so long.

'Let's get out of here,' I say, eager to finally feel safe again after what seems like an eternity on edge.

Sebastian doesn't argue this time. He got what he came for. Unfortunately, I doubt he intended on leaving with more questions than he had before.

We manage to exit the chamber and make our way back into the hallway without anyone noticing. I can't get away from the chambers quickly enough, and we've walked for several minutes before I feel safe enough to talk about what just happened.

'So what do you think?' I ask, when we turn down an empty corridor.

'I think you better start eating porridge with all the rationing that's about to begin in the North Wing.'

'You know that's not what I mean!'

Sebastian laughs, but the sound he makes is rigid and I can tell his thoughts are deeply focused on the stars we've just heard about.

'Be serious. What do you think this means?'

'I think things are about to change,' he answers cautiously.

'Change how?'

Sebastian stops walking and turns to me, before he quietly says, 'I don't know, I'm scared to even think the words. Let alone say them aloud.'

'You think we're going to return to the surface?' I whisper, looking over my shoulder to check the corridor is still empty.

His eyes flicker to mine before looking away. In that one glance I can see how desperately he wants it to be true. 'Yes,' he says simply.

A part of me wants to agree with him, but a larger part of me knows there's more to this. That a glimpse of the stars through the ravaged night skies isn't a clear signal the surface is changing.

'There has to be a reason they're covering it up though,' I say slowly, trying to be careful with my words so as not to upset the hope I see in Sebastian's eyes. 'They clearly don't want people to know about it. What if returning is not possible and that's why they're keeping it from us?'

Sebastian's shoulders slouch down in defeat. 'We don't know why they're keeping it secret. Maybe because it's still another few years before we can return?'

'Maybe.' I shrug as I turn to resume walking. I don't want to keep talking about something we can't change. It would almost be better if we didn't know at all, so we had no cause to wonder.

Both of us are silent as we head down the elaborate stairs of the West Wing and out across the Atrium. I'm sure Sebastian is coming up with a whole list of irrefutable counter arguments for why I'm wrong. My silence is heavier though, and a whole lot more troubling.

I fold my arms across my chest and chew down on my lower lip. There's a bad feeling in the pit of my stomach about what we've overheard. Sebastian may have joked about the food rationing, and we can't be sure what is happening on the surface, but I feel like he's right about one thing. Everything is about to change.

THE RICH AROMA of frying onions and garlic hits me as I enter the dining hall, causing the growling in my stomach to become an all out roar. It's almost as if it knows it's about to be fed, and is all the hungrier for it.

Sebastian goes to find us a table while I head straight for the food queue, which is thankfully short. I'm so hungry I'd probably eat porridge tonight.

As I make my way back from the food counter, he pulls out the chair next to him. 'What are the options?'

'Pasta again,' I say, placing my tray down on the table. 'I'm not even sure what the other stuff they were serving was.'

'Probably safer not to ask,' he jokes, as he gets up to join the food queue.

I chuckle and take my multivitamin tablets, swallowing them down with several large gulps of water. I quickly move onto the food, desperate to fill the gaping hole in my stomach—I will never be one of those girls who can get by on a lettuce leaf.

'So, where were you all day?' I ask when Sebastian returns with a tray of food. I'd intended to ask him earlier why he wasn't at school today, but he'd successfully managed to distract me with the Council Chambers.

'I wasn't feeling too well this morning, so stayed home.'

'Are you feeling any better?' I ask, curious as to whether I had anything to do with his 'sickness.' He seemed quite out of sorts when I left him this morning.

'Mmm,' he mumbles, as he takes a mouthful. 'I seem to be fine now.'

A peal of laughter rings through the room. I don't even need to look to know it belongs to Quinn. Her laughter rings again, louder this time. I glance over to see a guy whispering in her ear. Whatever he's saying must be hilarious because she's giggling uncontrollably. I wonder if that's the guy she went on a date with last night?

I focus on my plate as I try to twirl the pasta perfectly around my fork. 'So, you never said, how did you find that-uh-*room* you took me to?'

Sebastian shifts uncomfortably in his chair and focuses intently on his food.

I raise my eyebrows at him as he squirms. 'Seriously, how did you know it was there? And who helped you get clearance?' I persist.

Again my question is met with silence. 'Well?'

He opens his mouth to say something, but then stops. Instead he considers my plate. 'Are you done?'

I glance down at the few strings of pasta still on my plate. Before I can answer he stands and picks up both of our plates to take them to the kitchen.

'But I wasn't finished...' I reply, my response falling on deaf ears.

As I watch his rigid back walk towards the kitchen something feels off. I shake my shoulders, trying to relax, but it doesn't seem to help. I still feel uneasy, and the hairs on the back of my neck seem to prickle.

Disconcerted, I look around to find two warm, brown eyes watching me from across the room. Our eyes lock for a split second, before I quickly look down. I can feel myself flush, embarrassed.

Ryan is here.

My stomach drops several notches. It's been ages since I've seen him around.

Now I know he's watching, I can almost sense his gaze on me. Unable to help myself, I give in and look over. Again I find him watching and I find I can't look away.

His tanned skin is so unusual for someone who lives in the ARC, and combined with his long, dark tussled hair, he's gorgeous. Even the scar that runs through his eyebrow adds to his appearance.

It's not like I want him *that* way. Well, at least I don't want to like him *that* way. He's way too old for me. I guess the best way to explain it, is I feel a connection to him. We seem to understand each other.

He smiles at me and I automatically respond with a smile in return.

'Elle?' Sebastian's troubled voice comes from beside me.

Reluctantly I pull away from Ryan's captivating stare and turn to

Sebastian. He's focused on something over towards where Ryan sits and his eyes flick back to me as I turn to him.

'Did you want some dessert?' he asks, his voice unusually tight. 'They're doing carrot sticks tonight.'

I shake my head. He shrugs and turns back towards the kitchen. As he does I notice Ryan is no longer sitting across the room. I crane my neck, trying to see where he's gone, but he must have finished dinner and left. I slump down in my chair disappointed.

'Hi Elle,' a deep voice murmurs in my ear.

I jerk my body up straight in shock. I turn in my seat and watch as Ryan slides down into Sebastian's chair.

I go to reply, to come up with something clever and witty, but my mind draws a blank. 'Hey,' is the quiet and oh-so-lame response I come up with.

He edges the seat towards me. 'How've you been?' he asks, his tone light and conversational.

'Good,' I say, when nothing else springs to mind.

'Good's good.' He laughs in response.

'How are you?' I ask, my fingers restlessly playing with my pendant.

'I'm *good*. I'm happy I get to see you,' he says, looking deeply into my eyes. My heart skips a beat and my cheeks warm with delight.

I take a deep breath and try to calm down. I feel stupid reacting this way when he's obviously just being nice. He's old enough to be one of my teachers, and I'll admit sometimes our friendship does feel like that formal student-teacher relationship. Other times he relaxes and I think he forgets how much younger I am. It's then that I start to get bad ideas.

Ugh, I barely know the guy. I don't know what I'm thinking.

I notice Sebastian across the room talking to one of his friends. Their discussion looks heated and his eyes flicker this way several times.

'Sorry?' I ask, turning back to Ryan. I've completely missed what he's just said.

'I asked if you were doing much this week?'

'No,' I reply distracted. I catch another glimpse of Sebastian. He's no longer talking to his friend, but is walking out of the room. He looks in this direction just as he walks out the door, his face is completely dark and his eyes are seething with rage.

I turn back to Ryan and stand up as I say, 'I have to go. I'll catch you around?'

He looks surprised by the abrupt change in mood, but quickly recovers.

'Okay, well I'll see you soon.'

'Bye Ryan,' I say stumbling over my chair in my hurry to get up.

I leave the dining hall and jog down the hallway to try and catch up with Sebastian.

'Sebastian!' I call, when I see him up ahead. He doesn't turn back, but keeps walking.

'Sebastian, wait up!' I call louder. He stops and pauses for me.

'Hey,' I say, trying to catch my breath. I have to wait a few seconds before I can continue. 'What's up? Why'd you leave dinner so suddenly?'

'I'm surprised you even noticed. You looked pretty busy.'

'Well I wasn't.' I watch him, waiting for him to explain. He's acting really pissed off.

'You know what Elle? You don't need to know every detail of my life. There's this crazy concept called privacy. Heard of it?'

'I don't mean to pry. I just wanted to check you're okay.' I falter, surprised by his attack.

'Yeah well, just don't! You need to stop. Getting. In. My. Head!' He spits the words at me.

'Oh,' I say, taking a step back. 'Okay.' I step back further.

'Elle,' he says, lowering his voice, which is husky with frustration.

'It's fine.' I turn and start walking back down the hallway but hear a loud, splitting bang behind me. From the sounds of it he's kicked the wall, but I don't look back. He obviously doesn't need or want my help.

The walk home seems longer tonight and the whole way back I get the feeling I'm the reason Sebastian's angry. I rub at my eyes tiredly. I think it's been a big day for both of us. Hopefully we'll both get some sleep and everything will be okay in the morning. Unfortunately, it doesn't change how hurt I feel tonight.

When I get to my door, I put my hand in my pocket to grab my swipe key. As I bring it out a piece of paper falls on the floor. I bend over to pick it up as I make my way inside. The room is cold and empty. I doubt Quinn will be back for a while.

I place my swipe card down on the table, and unfold the piece of paper. I can't think of when I would've put it in my pocket and it's not the kind of thing I'd forget. Paper isn't exactly easy to come by in the ARC. You usually have to trade for it, even if it's a piece this small. I hate to think what Adam traded to get Sebastian his sketchbook.

I hold the small rectangle of paper up to the light to read it. The note is only short and when I finish I grip it firmly to my chest, not quite able to believe what it says. I'm unexpectedly excited for tomorrow.

I hurry to change and get into bed, determined to have a good night's sleep. Sleep evades me though, as images of star-streaked skies fill my mind. The sounds of my rapidly thudding heart and the gentle buzzing hum of the ARC are like the score to my excited musings, and it takes me a while to settle down.

Eventually I begin to drift off, and as I finally feel sleep's gentle pull beginning to overcome me, I feel a twinge of guilt. *How would Sebastian feel about what I plan to do in the morning?*

CHAPTER EIGHT

I wake with a start. A cold sweat covers my body, chilling me to the core. It's been such a long time since I've experienced such vivid nightmares.

Though my body is still cocooned in fear, I sit up and try to quell the spike of adrenaline that has roused inside me. *It was only a dream*, I try to remind myself.

All the same, the sight of Quinn asleep, curled in a ball under her sheets, a cascade of blonde hair tumbling down over them, is reassuring. *She's still here. She's not taken.*

I've always had nightmares of my friends being taken. I guess you'd be crazy not to. It's something that's always been a threat. This dream felt different though. It felt like something more than just fear, more like a menacing omen of what is to come.

I shudder and curl my arms around my knees. Maybe Quinn and Sebastian are right? I survey the room uneasily—almost expecting something to jump out of the shadows. In the soft blue hue of the night-light everything is more ominous.

A breathy laugh escapes me and I swing my legs off the bed. I really know how to freak myself out. I feel silly for being so pessimistic at such an early hour.

Yawning, I stand and quietly stretch, not wanting to disturb Quinn. I quickly get dressed and as I creep towards the door, being careful not to stumble in the dim room, I take the small piece of paper out of my pocket. I open it over by the small light that glows next to the door handle. My eyes focus on the four numbers written in faint, blue pen, 'four, three, five and nine.'

I read them again and again to commit them to memory. It's hard to concentrate on the numbers though when my eyes keep scanning to the name written at the bottom of the page. Ryan.

When I'm convinced I can retain the numbers, I tear the paper into small little pieces and put them in my pocket. As I place my hand on the door I can just make out the steady rhythm of Quinn's breathing. Reassured she's still asleep, I slip out of the room.

I rush down the corridors and quickly find myself where the more civilized quarters of the North Wing are located. You can tell they are nicer because there's an acrylic smell emanating from the freshly painted walls, and a distinct lack of spider webs.

It's still early and the corridors in this more populated section are relatively deserted. The few people I do cross are on their way to work in the kitchens; off to prepare another tasteless, nutrient-packed meal for the masses I'm sure.

I make my way to the Atrium, which is bustling with people. It's not really surprising, as it always seems to be busy in here. I take the exit that leads to the East Wing, where all ARC manufacturing and produce occurs.

As I enter the wing my pace quickens. It's as though my legs have a mind of their own and they know we're getting closer. I practically fly down the steps to one of the lower levels and only slow down when I reach the door that I'm after.

My heart is in my mouth and my hand shakes slightly as I lift it to the pin pad just above the door handle. With careful precision I enter the numbers 'four,' 'three,' 'five,' I suck in a breath, and 'nine'.

The light on the pin pad glows green. I exhale and push the door open.

Closing the door behind me, I turn and can feel my whole face light up as my eyes indulge in the sight before me.

I'm in a large room that extends as far as the eye can see. It must be at least four stories high, with huge round lamps that hang from the roof. Below them, metal suspended walkways network like an intricate spider's web just above my head.

And there, below the lights and under the walkways, an expanse of greenery grows. Neat and endless rows of vegetation shoot off into the distance, with the smallest of concrete pathways cutting between the leafy plants.

The air around me is thick with moisture. The earthy, fresh smell of mint combined with the rich, robust aroma of rosemary tingles at my nose, and the soft gentle trickle of sprinklers reaches my ears.

I am in the Plantation, my *favourite* place in the ARC.

I take a moment to revel in the calm, exotic atmosphere of the place. Then I set off into the greenery. I know I don't have much time before the workers clock on for the day and there's no way I plan on getting caught. I have to act fast if I want to reach the far corner of the vast garden in time. I don't need to search, or mindlessly wander through the endless rows of plants though. I already know exactly where Ryan will be.

When I reach the olive grove I catch my first glimpse of the apple orchard that lies just beyond. It is glorious, and as always the trees are covered in the shiny red fruit. Below one of the large trees, set slightly apart from the others, stands a man cloaked in shadow. Ryan. He's standing waiting for me and I find my stride naturally lengthens, the closer that I get.

As I reach him he tosses an apple to me. I catch it, laugh and take a bite. The first taste is ecstasy as the sweet crisp juice drizzles through my mouth. I find I have to stop myself from groaning out loud in delight.

I can't even remember the last apple I'd tasted. *Maybe Christmas?*

I wonder. Unfortunately, the more indulgent, perishable food is saved for those in the ARC of higher importance. After talk of further rationing in the Council meeting last night, I can't be certain I'll get to taste another one any time soon.

'Hey Elle,' Ryan says, as he reaches up to pluck another apple from the tree. He's smiling, but under the bright lamps his face seems lined with worry.

'Ryan,' I muffle, placing my hand over my mouth in an attempt to disguise the apple I still munch on.

'I was worried you weren't going to come.' He's looking down at his own half-eaten apple, and his face creases as though he's bothered by the thought.

'And miss out on this?' I say, taking a second decisive bite of my apple. 'No way.'

He laughs and eases himself down onto the grass that grows under the tree. 'How's school?' he asks, as I sit down on the ground next to him.

I raise my eyebrows at him and ignore the question. He knows I don't want to talk about school. He's thirteen years older than me; he could hardly be interested in how I went in my latest math's test.

'Okay, no school talk.' He looks at me more seriously. 'Your testing is coming up soon. Isn't it?'

I stare back at him and struggle to respond. Testing, *such a testy topic*. I've only just gotten past the stress of Quinn's testing and I don't particularly want to talk about my own.

My fingers begin to restlessly pull at the grass that tickles my fingertips. 'Yes. I have my testing in a few weeks,' I admit.

'You'll be fine,' he reassures me. 'There's nothing for you to worry about.' It's nice of him to say, but he really doesn't have to. I'm fine with being tested. It's everyone else getting tested that scares me senseless.

'You probably shouldn't be in here with me, but I couldn't help myself. I know how much you love this place.'

He's right; I *do* love this place. I imagine it's the closest thing to the surface, before impact, I might ever get to see. I mean yeah, we do have the virtual reality simulators, but they only give you a visual of what surface life used to be. At least here in the Plantation you can feel the moisture in the air, smell the freshness of the plants.

'Do you ever wonder if maybe we could return to the surface?' I ask him.

He frowns and looks at the ground around us, as though searching for another apple. 'Why do you ask that?' His words are slow and seem carefully chosen.

I consider telling him about what I overheard in the Council Chambers, but immediately disregard it. I'm not even certain what Ryan does for the ARC and I don't want to get Sebastian or myself in trouble.

'I just wondered.' I shrug.

He glances up at me, his curious eyes probing me for answers, before turning away to continue his search for fallen apples. 'When the surface becomes sustainable again for people, they will return to it,' he says, confidently.

I watch Ryan closely. His eyes are guarded and it seems like he's holding back. I can't tell if he knows something or if he is simply recounting the same lines we've always been told. The way he's acting though, I think it's safe to assume he knows more.

'Is there something I'm missing?' I ask.

I receive no response to this. He simply shakes his head and looks up, laughter replacing the restrained look in his eyes.

The reaction reminds me so much of our first meeting—well, first collision. It was about a year ago. I'd been walking through the dining hall juggling both Quinn's food tray and mine when I bumped into him. Literally. I was so focused on the trays of food I ploughed straight into him.

His hands were quick to steady me as I lost my footing, and miraculously I didn't lose anything from my trays. I looked up to apologise for my idiocy, but my brain turned to mush and, for a second, time seemed to stand still.

He had shaken his head just like he's doing now, and his eyes danced with amusement. He helped me rebalance my items, then without a word walked right past me.

In my state of shock, I failed to string two words together. He was good looking, yes, but that wasn't what really stopped me in my tracks. It was what I'd seen in his eyes. They had been so bright and playful, with what felt like a hint of recognition. By the time I'd found my tongue again and turned to say thanks, he had gone.

Ryan still sits there amused. His eyes finally land on an apple. He stretches his arm right out to grab it, and begins rubbing it on his trousers before popping it in his pocket.

'Ryan,' I say. 'Am I missing something?' I still can't shake the feeling he's keeping something from me.

'No,' he responds, almost to himself, the smile falling from his face. He stands abruptly, and walks a few steps away, out of the shadow of the tree. I quietly get up to follow him, uncertain why his mood has changed so suddenly

'You should go,' he says. His voice is calm and distant. 'You've got school to get to. Plus you need to leave before the farmers come to work for the day. I won't have you getting into trouble on my account.' He takes a deep breath before he continues. 'I'm not going to be back for a while.'

I turn away from him and bow my head. Every time is the same; he will suddenly turn up and then just as quickly he will disappear again for months on end. He is constantly leaving. I can only guess at what he's doing, but he won't tell me, and I will no longer ask.

'Okay,' I say quietly. 'I understand.' He grabs a hold of my shoulder and gives it a reassuring squeeze.

Why must he be constantly leaving? I like our talks, but it feels like they're becoming few and far between.

I turn back around to say goodbye, but he's already gone.

CHAPTER NINE

I'm running late and I can only blame myself.

After I left the apple tree I was distracted. My thoughts were so tangled, obsessing over the mystery that is Ryan, I nearly ran into several farmers. It was only through sheer luck I managed to avoid them. I ended up having to hide in a pumpkin patch while they stood there having a good old chat. They'd just arrived for the day and were attempting to delay starting work, so it felt like they talked there forever.

I spent the entirety of my time hiding fuming at myself. If I had been concentrating I would have heard them a mile away and chosen a different path.

Eventually they moved on and I continued my race to get to school on time. The hallways were crazy busy. It was that time of day when it seemed like everyone in the ARC had somewhere to be. The Atrium alone took me five minutes to get through.

When I finally make it to the school lobby, I'm puffing like I've just played a full game of basketball. Luckily, the large bright room still has students milling around in it, so I've made it in time.

'Elle!' I hear my name called. 'Over here!'

Sebastian waves at me from the far side of the room. I frown and approach him very cautiously. He seems to be acting like last night didn't happen and this has me feeling very tense.

He's standing out the front of the English classroom chatting animatedly to some girl who I only vaguely recognise. I think she's in his year, but I've never spoken to her. Well, whoever she is, she seems to be engrossed in whatever he is telling her.

As I approach I hear him say, 'Well I guess I'll catch you later Chelsea.' Her shoulders slouch with disappointment as she is effectively dismissed. Sebastian turns to me, remorse evident on his face.

'Elle...' he begins, apologetically.

'What do you want Sebastian?' I dig my hands into my pockets and rock on the backs of my shoes.

'I'm sorry. I was out of line last night.' I watch him quietly, allowing him space to explain. 'I was just in a bad place and I seriously overreacted.'

Trying to kick a hole in the wall seems to go way beyond overreacting.

He scratches his head, concern furrowing his brow. 'Listen, I just wanted you to know that I realise I shouldn't have taken my own issues out on you.'

'No you shouldn't have. I still don't even know what you were upset about.' He shifts uneasily as I stare at him, waiting for him to explain.

'I don't want to talk about it,' he mutters uncomfortably.

'Well I think I deserve to know, given the way you acted towards me. Did I do something wrong?'

He doesn't respond.

'Were you angry because I questioned you about finding that room?' I ask quietly, admitting what I fear is the problem.

'No, of course not. Honestly Elle, I was being stupid. It's nothing.'

I cross my arms, waiting for an explanation, not believing he would ever act the way he did over nothing.

He ignores my crossed arms and obvious disbelief, and gives me his most charming smile. 'So, friends?' he asks.

'Are you really not going to explain what this is all about?'

He slowly shakes his head. 'I'm sorry about last night, really I am. Please will you forgive me?'

I sigh and unfold my arms. He's turning all of his charm on me this morning and it's hard enough to resist at the best of times. I feel my will to be angry with him dissolve. 'Well are you planning on arguing with me again anytime soon?'

'Of course not.'

'Then I guess we can be friends. But I'm still upset you'd lash out at me the way you did. And, well, just no more freak-outs! Okay?' I'm way too easy on this guy.

He laughs in response. 'I think I can agree to that.'

We stand in uncomfortable silence for a minute.

'So who was that girl you were talking to before?' I ask, trying to act like things are back to normal.

'Who Chelsea? She's just a girl in my year,' he responds.

'She's cute, and she seems interested. Are you going to take her on a date?'

He looks down at his feet and shuffles them. 'She's just a friend. Besides, I'm waiting for *the one*,' he says in an attempt to joke, but I swear his cheeks are turning pink.

'Oh, by the way, I have something for you,' I say, as the bell for class rings overhead.

'What, even though I'm a psycho?'

'Yes, even though you're a psycho.'

He looks up intrigued. Are his eyes a brighter shade of blue today? As I look into them, the tingling I'd felt the other night awakens, and I can feel it slowly building in my stomach. I glare down at it accusingly. *If you don't stop that, I will punch you,* I warn it.

He looks at me as if to say, 'I'm waiting,' so I quickly rush on.

'But not until lunch. And not here,' I lower my voice to a

murmur, 'Let's meet in the archives.' I know no one will see what I've brought for him there.

'The archives,' he repeats. 'Okay. Till then!' He winks and walks through the door to his English class.

I turn back around to the foyer, which is now slowly emptying of students, and head across to the history classroom. I'm incredulous; how has he managed to wiggle his way back onto my good side with such ease? That boy should give lessons! Then again, I've never been able to stay angry with him.

I spot Gemma towards the back of the room and I head to the seat next to hers.

'You'll never guess what happened to me last night!' she exclaims, as I approach.

'Let me guess ... Cam?' I say with a laugh, as I pull my chair out and take a seat. It's hardly a guessing game.

'Yep,' she says proudly. 'He took me on a date.' She says it as though she hardly believes it herself. They've been flirting for long enough though, she shouldn't be so surprised.

'Where did you guys go?'

'Well he's been doing his community service hours at the cinema and I guess he's become quite friendly with the manager there. He talked him into letting us have the cinema to ourselves to watch a movie.'

'That's amazing!'

'I know. It was very unexpected. He only asked me once everyone left basketball.'

'How was your mum about it?' I ask delicately. Her mum can be an absolute nightmare.

'Pissed, as you can imagine. I wasn't home until late.'

'How late?' I ask.

She blushes in reply. 'Late...'

'Gemma!' I gently thump her arm.

'What? We just kissed a bit...'

'A bit? I can see the hickey from here!'

'What!' The colour drains from her face and she grabs the side of her neck.

I burst out laughing. She's too easy to fool.

'So not funny Elle,' she says, thumping my arm in return.

Ms. Matthews enters the room, and the chatty hubbub of the class quietens. I lean back in my chair, still smiling, and get ready to switch my mind off. I find spacing out is harder than usual today though, and my interest is piqued when Ms. Matthews opens the case she carries to reveal a virtual projector.

You can almost feel the contagious buzz of excitement spread through the classroom when she announces that today we are focusing on the world just before the day of impact.

She turns the projector on and the entire room is engulfed in images. We are immersed in simulations of tall majestic buildings and large burgeoning cities. Forests that are green, lush and alive buzz with activity. Tall ancient oaks stand strong, untouched for an age and a surreal atmosphere is created under a canopy of trees, as subdued light flickers through the leaves.

Students sit forward in their seats when a simulation of a beach surrounds us. It is bathed in the orange and purple glow of the sun setting along the endless horizon. Even Ms. Matthews' bored face lights up as she gazes at the sun. She at least can remember the feel of its warmth across her skin and I can't decide whether that's better or worse.

As the image flicks to a towering mountain, cloaked in an eerie mist, I shudder. My whole body begins shaking and feels as though it's been fully submerged in the ice that clings to the rocky peak. My own memories of a different mountain arise and my thoughts are helplessly captured by them. My eyes no longer see the virtual simulations and instead I am surrounded by the one day I never want to think about.

There is screaming, so much screaming, as people fight their way past each other, desperate to find their way to the front of the mob. The adults all tower over me and from this far away it's impossible to see the huge dark gate carved into the side of the mountain. I know exactly where it is though. Everyone is desperate to be one the few refugees to make their way across its threshold, so they all rush frantically towards it.

Most people seem terrified, clinging to their loved ones as they attempt to protect them. But it is nothing compared to the complete fear I feel welling up inside me. My parents are gone, I have no idea where, and I am alone in a world submerged in crying and shoving and panicked screams.

The sound is all too familiar and even now, years later, I can still remember the screams with remarkable clarity. This is one of the few, flickering memories I have from before impact. It has haunted me over the years, almost as much as the half-formed impressions of warmth and love I have from before that.

The others stare longingly at the simulation, but my hands clench as I wait for it to be turned off. The bell finally chimes for lunch and we all quietly pack our tablets back into our bags. In silent contemplation we head for the door and everyone spills out into the busy foyer. The crowd is a far cry from my memories of the day of impact. It's more like the ocean simulation I watched earlier, one strong but calm surge towards the dining hall. I tell Gemma I'll catch her later and then slip between the other students to make my way into the library.

As I enter the archive room I gently close the door behind me. Sebastian sits on the floor, behind one of the library stacks, his back propped up against the wall. He closes the book on his lap as I walk over.

'A bit of light reading?' I ask. The book in his hands is *huge*.

He wiggles it up in the air. 'You just wish you had the patience to get through a whole book,' he retorts.

I screw my nose up at him. As I do, I glance at the cover of the book, 'Post Apocalypse: The Lysart Asteroid's Effect on the Surface,' the title says.

'You're reading through all that surface literature again?' I thought he'd given up on all the conspiracy theories that used to circulate.

'I was just flicking while I waited,' he says, somewhat embarrassed.

A picture of the barren surface covers the front of the book. It makes me sad to think all those beautiful places I'd just seen in class have been lost.

'Sebastian, you can't keep looking through these books hoping to find a mistake in them. We all know there's nothing up there anymore.'

'What about the stars Elle? Like you said, there has to be a reason they're covering it up.'

'It was probably a freak occurrence and they don't want people to get false hope. Look at the way you've reacted. You're straight back to believing there's something up there.'

He shakes his head passionately. 'That's not true. I've always thought there was more up there than the wastes we see on our screens. The Earth is huge, and I don't believe that one asteroid alone could take everything out.'

I groan, frustrated. 'You know it didn't. It was the impact winter that did most of the damage.'

He sits there thinking for a moment. 'Well there has to be something up there,' he replies quietly. 'How else will I be able to find Mum and April?' There is absolute loss and agony in his voice as he says this, and it takes everything in me not to say the easy, reassuring answer: that of course there's life up there; that his mum and April are living happily on the surface.

'Sebastian, you know I want them to be alive more than anything, but you've seen the live feeds. Even if for a brief moment the clouds opened and the stars were seen, it doesn't mean it's any different up there. If it were, why would they lie to us? Why wouldn't we be back living above ground? It just doesn't make sense!'

'Yeah, you're right,' he responds, his shoulders slouching in defeat. 'I guess it's just that I still miss them, and there's a part of me that has to believe there's something more than this.' He waves his arms around the room.

'I know, me too.' I walk over to the wall and slide down next to him. 'You know, just because there's nothing up there, doesn't mean they're not somewhere safe.'

There's no way of knowing where they are, so we can only ever speculate. I watch his face, as he stares thoughtfully at the far end of the archive room. He then turns to me, his face now only inches away, his blue eyes looking deeply into mine.

'We're older now. Safe or not, I don't think I could just stay here and allow you to be taken away from me. If they took you from me I would come for you,' he whispers intensely.

I stare back at him, shocked. It's such a controversial thing to think, let alone say aloud. People are quarantined for a reason. If he came after me, he'd surely become tainted too.

As I look into his eyes I can see his determination and resolve. He won't have another person taken away from him. His face begins to drop when I don't respond and he goes to look away. I lightly take a hold of his chin and pull it back so he looks me in the eye.

'I don't think I could just let you go either. I'd come for you too,' I whisper back.

He beams in response, but his eyes are fierce, as though he'd take on every person in the ARC to keep me safe.

'Promise?' he says.

'Promise.'

He laughs to lighten the mood and then focuses down on the book in his hands. 'I've been wanting to talk to you about something,' he says, refusing to look at me.

'You have?'

'Yeah.'

'Well—what is it?' I ask when he doesn't continue.

A frown crosses his face. 'It's about us,' he starts uneasily.

'Okay...' I laugh uncomfortably. Where the hell is he going with this?

'Do you remember a few weeks ago when that massive group of us met in the rec room late at night?'

'The night we played spin the bottle?'

'Yeah.'

'What about it?' I ask. My heart is thumping so loudly I begin to worry he can hear it. I think I know what he wants to talk about and I have a sudden wish to just disappear.

'I wanted to ask you why you refused to kiss me when it landed on us?'

I freeze, feeling completely unsure how to respond. I don't even know why I refused to at the time. I acted like a complete idiot that night and the last thing I want to do is relive it.

'I guess because you're my best friend,' I say. 'I can't kiss you and risk losing that.'

'It was just a stupid kiss,' he mutters.

I shrug and refuse to talk about it any further. The whole thing was embarrassing then and it's just as embarrassing for me now.

He watches me cautiously. 'Don't you want to why I'm—'

'Oh, I nearly forgot. Your surprise.' I cut him off. I pull my bag onto my lap and start to forage through it.

'Elle, I think I should tell—'

'Do you want your surprise or not?' I ask him.

He sighs and nods. I don't know why he'd want to dwell on that night anyway.

'Now close your eyes. Put out your hands. And ta da!' He opens his eyes and his face lights up.

'Strawberries!' he exclaims. 'But how did you—' He stops mid-sentence, a scowl crossing his face. 'You went to the Plantation again.' His words are an accusation rather than a question.

'It's not like you haven't done it before.'

'I know, but I thought we'd both agreed to stop. It's dangerous.' Pretty rich coming from a guy who had me break into the Council Chambers, not even 24 hours earlier.

'It was fine.' I try to reassure him, but he looks so worried.

He goes quiet for several minutes and I wait silently for his anger to subside. When he does speak again, disappointment is rife in his voice. 'You went with *him* again. Didn't you?' he says.

I have no idea what he's talking about so I wait for him to explain.

'Ryan. You met him in the Plantation again.'

'Yes. And?' I reply, confused. I don't know why it's such a big deal.

'He's *old*! You shouldn't hang out with him.'

'He's not *that* old,' I counter. He's totally too old to hang out with, but there's no way I'm letting Sebastian know I agree with him. I stand and swing my bag onto my shoulder. 'You know what, I should probably go get some lunch. You coming?'

Sebastian glances down at the book closed on the floor next to him. 'Nah, I have a few things I want to check up on in the library. I'll see you later.'

Sebastian's behaviour is worrying me, yet I leave him to his 'things' in the library. I am still mulling over why he's acting so strange when I reach the school dining hall. I'm so worried about Sebastian, it takes me a minute to realise everyone is quiet. Not quite silent but they are all muttering in hushed voices to each other. Something is definitely up.

I grab a tray and line up to get some food. I peer around as I wait, attempting to figure out what's going on. Kate stands in line in front of me chatting dramatically to a couple of her friends. I take a step closer and try to overhear what she's saying. I manage to catch the end of a sentence.

'...had been mixing with the wrong people. So I guess who knows?' she says. Kate's good at commanding her audience. She lets that settle over the girls before she continues. 'And to think I saw her out in the foyer just before talking to Sebastian.'

'What did she look like?' one of the enthralled girls asks.

'Oh, well, you could definitely tell the girl was sick. She was sweating all over and, to be honest, I thought she was about to faint. I guess she was really nervous about her testing?' The girls both nod in agreement. 'But to think,' she pauses for dramatic effect, 'she was *tainted*!' The two girls gasp.

'Sorry,' I interrupt. 'Kate, who are you talking about? What's happened?'

'Oh Elle.' She turns to me and recoils like there's a bad smell under her nose. 'Have you been sitting under a rock all lunch?'

I ignore her jab at me. 'What's happened?' I repeat.

'Chelsea Turner,' she says, with a cruel snigger. 'She's been taken.'

CHAPTER TEN

We've always been told taking people is a necessary evil. They're sick and are unable to stay here because it threatens the safety of everyone else in the ARC.

No one knows why it affects some people and not others. All the Council will tell us is people become sick because of the new element brought to earth by the asteroid.

There were protests in the beginning, when people first started disappearing, but it rarely happens now. There are stories about the brutal things the Council did to make sure people complied. I'm not certain I believe the rumours are true though.

They tell us taking the tainted away is for their own good. I personally like to believe people who are taken live in the top levels of the ARC. We can't access the top floors, so it makes sense. I guess that's why I've always been fascinated by trying to make out the figures that wander across the walkways high above the Atrium.

Maybe I'm naive to believe they're still alive, but my gut tells me the tainted are okay.

It has been ages since anyone from the ARC has been taken, and even longer since anyone from school has been taken. The morose atmosphere that seems to descend on the ARC when someone is found tainted is inescapable and all encompassing.

Classes are cancelled for the rest of the day, and students are invited to visit with the school therapist. The therapy sessions are a total waste of time, but they're mandatory for anyone close to someone who is taken.

As I leave the dining hall I see Sebastian exiting the library at the same time. There's pain so transparent in his eyes and his shoulders are hunched over as though his backpack weighs a thousand tonnes.

He doesn't notice me as he slowly turns to leave school. I take a step forward to follow him, to see if he's okay, but the look I saw on his face makes me hesitate. He disappears around the corner before I can make up my mind.

'Are you alright Elle?' I turn around to see Gemma coming up behind me. Her face is pale and, like most people who pass me in the foyer, she looks worried.

'Oh,' I scratch my head, 'Yeah.'

'Have you heard?' she asks, swallowing tightly, as though dreading the idea of repeating what's happened.

I nod in response. 'I can't believe it. No one's been taken in six months.'

'Has it really been that long? Poor Chelsea,' she says, causing a group of girls to burst into tears as they walk past and hear her name.

'Let's go to the sports centre,' I suggest. 'I doubt anyone would be in there right now.'

As we walk to the gym I become frustrated and annoyed by how shallow most of the kids around me are. I understand Chelsea's friends must be grieving, but half the students I come across are gossiping, the other half are acting devastated, despite never knowing her.

I can feel my teeth clenching as we walk past a large group of younger girls. One particularly obnoxious girl laughs as she says, 'I always knew there was something *wrong* about her...'

Gemma firmly grabs my arm and tugs me away from the group as

I turn to give the girl a piece of my mind. I may not have known Chelsea, but she definitely doesn't deserve being talked about with such disrespect.

'Elle, don't...' Gemma warns as she firmly marches me away. I relax my shoulders and allow her to steer me around another group of students, who are huddled together, comforting each other.

Finally we arrive at the gym. I begin to relax as we enter the large, empty space. Gemma insists we sit on the trampolines and as soon as we sit down, and I allow the gentle bouncing momentum to rock me, I can see the appeal. It's soothing and all my muscles slacken as I allow myself to unwind.

'Intense day,' Gemma says, while she scoops her dark blonde hair back into a ponytail. 'I barely knew the girl. Still, I wouldn't want to be in her place right now.' She lies back and stares at the ceiling. 'Did you know her well?'

'I've seen her face around, but I wouldn't say I knew her,' I admit. 'I saw her talking to Sebastian this morning. I think they were friends.' I try not to sound like that troubles me, but I'm worried about how he's coping after seeing him looking so sad before. 'I really hope he's not taking it too hard.'

'Don't worry about it Elle, I'm sure he's fine.' she says.

I try to feel reassured by what she's said, but it makes me want to check in on him even more.

'Did you hear about the dance?' Gemma asks.

'What about it?'

'They're moving it up to this Saturday!' she says, unable to keep the excitement from her voice. 'There was a notice on the board about it at lunch. They must have decided it would be a good pick-me-up for the students after what's happened with Chelsea. I mean, it has been so long since anyone's been taken, it's really shaken everyone up.' She pauses, thinking. 'I just hope I don't end up in something as bad as what I wore last time!'

I nod sympathetically. Gemma's outfit at the last dance had been pretty atrocious. It was some gaudy number with sequins all over it.

Mine hadn't been too bad, a simple blue dress. Of course Kate had managed to wear the most amazing outfit. A red, backless dress that had all the boys drooling. Then again, she's a councilman's daughter and has resources far beyond those of the school costume room.

'You really had no chance of getting a good one with that unfair detention. It's seriously not your fault,' I say. 'Don't even worry about your outfit for a second. I will personally make certain we find you a good one this time!'

She seems slightly encouraged by this.

I'm about to start scheming on how we can make certain we are the first in line tomorrow after school, when we hear a mixture of boys voices and the slapping of balls against the floor in the courts next door to the gym.

We both tilt our heads attempting to put names to voices, but are unable to make out what boys are there. I shrug my shoulders at Gemma and relax back on the trampoline. I'm not really bothered about knowing who's next door, but she seems to have different ideas. She hops off the trampoline and starts walking towards the door. As she nears, she turns and waves me over.

'Fine,' I whisper back to her. I don't even know why I'm whispering. I really don't care what boys are in the sports centre. She probably wants to know if it's Cam.

We both walk quietly to the gymnasium door. From here we can make out everything they say. I still have no idea who it is, but Gemma seems seriously intrigued.

I am leaning against the wall, my arms crossed against my body, when my ears perk up. I've just heard Sebastian's name.

'The kid was devastated when I told him about Chelsea,' one of the guys says.

'Well, do you blame him?' another responds. 'I would be too...'

I hold my breath, not daring to move. Gemma looks at me, concern crossing her face as I feel the blood drain from mine. Why is Sebastian *so* upset about Chelsea being taken?

My cuff vibrates with an incoming comm from Sebastian. I don't want to talk to him right now though, so I ignore it. Instead, I turn to Gemma and quietly tell her I'm leaving.

The guys are still chatting about Sebastian, but I tune them out. I'm not sure I want to know why Sebastian is devastated about Chelsea. The thought that something could have been going on between them leaves me feeling empty inside.

When I turn down my corridor I find Sebastian sitting by my door. He's leaning his back against it and staring up at the flickering light bulb that hangs precariously from the ceiling. His eyes seem deep in thought and my stomach clenches when I guess he's thinking of Chelsea.

'You didn't answer my comm,' he accuses as I approach.

I shrug and search my pockets for my swipe key. 'I was busy.' I try to avoid looking at him as I move past him to the door. The lock happily beeps and the door to my quarters opens.

'Are you too busy to talk now?' he asks, standing just inside the doorway, leaning against the frame.

My bag lands loudly on the floor as I drop it down, and I take a deep breath before turning back to him. 'No. Now's okay. What's up?'

He checks up and down the hallway before entering the room, closing the door behind him. 'I've been thinking a lot about what we heard last night. I want to know more about what they're hiding from us. It's clear they're keeping so many secrets and I think it's about time we knew the truth about the tainted.'

I sit down on my bed and cross my legs, pulling my hair to one side so I can play with its ends. I've also been thinking about last night all day and I want to know more too, but it's risky to keep breaking the rules in search of more information. Especially when the truth may make no difference anyway. 'We already know too much and I don't want to get into trouble senselessly searching for more information. I wouldn't even know where to start.'

Sebastian sits on Quinn's bed, all the while watching me, his eyes cautious as though he's evaluating me in some way. 'I think I know a way to get to the top levels of the ARC,' he says.

'Yeah right.'

'No really, I think I've found a way to the top of the ARC,' he repeats.

I stare at him, allowing his words to sink in. For as long as I can remember I've felt connected to the top levels of the ARC, like they have a magnetic pull over me. They've always seemed to elusively hold the answers I've searched for. Has he completely lost the plot though? There's no way to get up there unless he plans to somehow scale the Atrium walls. Surely any plan he's thought of is suicide.

'Does she really mean that much to you?' I finally ask.

'Who?'

'Chelsea. She's the reason you're doing this, isn't she?'

'What?' he exclaims with disbelief. 'Why would you ever think this is about Chelsea?'

'Well, it's only now she's gone you've come up with this plan.'

'Elle, trust me, this has nothing to do with Chelsea. I need to try and find the truth. I need to know what happened to my family, what could one day happen to us. Will you please come with me?'

I pause and fold my arms across my chest. With no one taken in over six months I'd slowly begun to feel safe here. The bad memories of constantly losing friends and family, and the fear of being taken myself, had slowly dissipated. Part of me had started to think maybe the danger had passed, that maybe people weren't going to get sick any longer.

Then last night, when I heard about the stars, I had dared to feel optimistic. Dared to dream that maybe there was hope for us yet. With Chelsea taken only hours ago it's clear I was a fool to feel hopeful. If Quinn was right, and a wave of people are about to be taken, we are in more danger than ever.

It's becoming clearer and clearer we can't just keep waiting around until another one of us falls sick and disappears. We have to uncover the truth the Council have so obviously hidden from us for our entire lives. I just worry the truth is far worse than we've ever imagined.

'How are you even going to get up there?' I ask.

'As part of my engineering apprenticeship I've been studying the schematics of the ARC. There's this old maintenance shaft that runs between all of the levels over in the East Wing. I suspect it goes all the way to the top.'

'Surely they would know about it?'

'I don't think so. They make new plans every couple of years of the ARC and I've been crosschecking between them all. There's only one plan that even mentions the shaft and it's from way back when the ARC was first built, before impact even occurred. I don't think anyone's used it since then.'

I shiver and rub my hands along my arms. Some old abandoned maintenance shaft sounds dangerous, like the kind of thing you'd expect teens to find in a horror flick. I also suspect it's likely to be dark and small, not exactly my favourite combination. 'It doesn't sound very safe,' I grumble.

'I'll look after you,' Sebastian says, with confidence. He falters though when he looks me in the eyes. 'But if you're not sure, I won't hold it against you if you want to stay behind.'

'I'm just nervous about the shaft,' I admit. 'But, that's not enough to stop me. Do you really think I'd give up the chance to see the top levels? I'm coming with you. Even though it will probably kill us both.'

Sebastian laughs and takes a hold of my hand. 'Are you sure?'

I laugh and try to ignore the way my hand tingles in his. Taking a deep breath I pull my hand free and step towards the door. 'No, definitely not, so we better leave before I come to my senses.'

CHAPTER ELEVEN

The shaft is the type of thing my worst nightmares are made of. The small metallic chute is only just larger than an average-sized man and the rusted metal ladder that can be seen in the dim light of Sebastian's torch looks ready to crumble with the lightest touch.

I glance down at the time on my cuff and shiver. Midnight. I shouldn't be surprised it's so late; it took us a lot longer to get to the shaft than we'd expected. The whole section of the wing has fallen into disuse and the massive room that houses the shaft appears to be some sort of communal dumping ground for all the unwanted things in the ARC.

The large, dark space is crammed to the brim with mounds of broken, abandoned items. It took us some time to make our way over the old, lifeless machinery and to shift the assortment of cracked bedheads and beaten up cupboards, to find our way to the back of the room.

Despite all that effort, I was secretly pleased when we finally found the small metal door to the shaft had rusted shut after so many years of disuse.

I probably should've packed it in then. I'd always known the shaft wasn't going to be my cup of tea and it was a perfectly reasonable excuse to give up. Sebastian is uncannily handy though, and it only took him several minutes to do some nifty work with a crowbar to open the door to the world's smallest manhole.

'I'm not going in there,' I say, shaking my head. 'No way. No how. No.' There is no light in the shaft and I can barely see two feet up or down it from the light that spills in from the room. 'You could've told me your precious schematics showed a tiny tunnel to hell. It would've saved me the trip out here.'

'I didn't realise it would be quite so small,' Sebastian admits. 'But on the upside we're only a couple of floors down from the top. We'll be in and out of there so quickly.'

I try to let his words calm me, but the thought of going in there has my blood running cold and my body freezing up. 'Let's just get this over with,' I mutter, my words braver than I feel.

Sebastian shines the beam of his torch inside the shaft. 'Do you want to go first or should I?' he asks, leaning in to look down it. The drop in there is endless and my stomach plummets at the thought of climbing up some dodgy old ladder.

'I'll go first,' I say, desperate to just get it over with already.

I take a firm grip of the rungs on the ladder before stepping my feet onto the ones below.

'You're doing great.'

'Haven't gone anywhere yet,' I respond through clenched teeth. Taking long breaths I start to slowly climb upwards. I can hear Sebastian close behind me as we make our way higher.

My hands feel sweaty and I worry constantly about losing my grip. I'm terrified, but the terror seems to push me forward rather than freeze me up. I know the only way to be safe again is to get out of here, so I keep moving forward with determination.

'Elle, stop. I think you're by the hatch now.' I look over my shoulder to find a small door behind me. 'Do you see that lever?'

I nod. It's red and quite large, so it would be hard to miss even without Sebastian shining his torch directly on it.

'Okay, now I want you to very carefully reach out with one hand and pull on it.'

'You want me to do what?'

'You need to open it up so we can get out,' Sebastian explains.

'Right,' I respond, my voice quivering. I loop one arm around the ladder to hold myself securely in place and reach across the gap between the ladder and the door with the other. My fingers only just grasp the handle so I have to lean out further to get a hold of it.

My whole body feels heavy and I'm fairly certain my stomach has abandoned ship, deciding instead to plunge into the depths of the bottomless shaft. I attempt to wrench the handle down, but it won't budge.

'It's stuck!' I panic.

'Just try it again,' Sebastian suggests calmly.

I gulp and lean out further trying to put more muscle behind it as I pull down on the handle. 'No it's definitely stuck,' I gasp, pulling back to the safety of the ladder.

'Should we try the next level up?' Sebastian asks.

I peer up into the darkness above, and am surprised to see the ceiling to the shaft several feet above us.

'We're at the top,' I call down to Sebastian.

I hear him grunt in response and mumble about it not making sense.

'So what do we do?' I ask, beginning to panic when he doesn't respond.

I feel Sebastian's arms grab the rungs by my legs. 'Let me have a try at the door. Can you move up a few steps?'

'Yeah, but first just give me one more shot,' I respond, feeling a sudden rush of resolve. This time when I reach out I feel surer of myself. Putting as much force into it as I dare, I pull down on the lever and feel the smallest movement.

'It's starting to go,' Sebastian says, as I wrench on the thing harder.

After a few more hefty tugs it thankfully begins to move. There's a loud groaning sound that echoes down the shaft, as the lever pulls down further.

'I did it!' I say excitedly, when the door swings open. It will only open slightly as it knocks against something heavy on the other side. It's a wide enough opening though that I should be able to fit through easily.

I look down at Sebastian grinning, but am confronted by the long drop I have to cross over to get out of here. My stomach lurches and I quickly snap my head back up to look at the door. I'm so desperate to get out of the shaft, but I can feel my fear surging again.

I stare resolutely at the door, refusing to look down, as I reach one arm and leg out across the gap to the safety of the room. My hand is shaky as it grasps onto the frame of the hatch and while I may not be looking down, my whole body is fully aware of the empty space below.

Taking one deep breath, I fling myself across and barrel my way into the dark and foreign room. Only moments later I hear Sebastian swear as he emerges after me himself.

Dim blue lights light the room and my eyes are slow to adjust. It's difficult to tell where I am until Sebastian lifts his torch and shines it around the room. It lands on long white sheets that have been draped over objects of various different sizes.

'Where are we?' I ask quietly.

Sebastian moves closer to one of the sheets and throws it off. A puff of dust is tossed into the air and the small specks of dirt flicker as they hover in the beam of light shooting from the torch. Sebastian clears his throat and shines the torch onto the imposing wooden desk he has revealed.

A computer monitor sits on top of it and stacks of manila files are piled over the remaining space. Sebastian moves closer and picks up one of the folders, opening it to inspect further.

'What's in there?' I ask, coughing as I inhale some of the dust.

'It's a file on someone,' he says, flicking through the pages. 'Test results I think.'

I instinctively take a step closer so I can peer over his arm at the open folder.

Sebastian glances over to me before his eyes continue skimming over the page. 'His name is Simon Ward and he lives in the West Wing. Well, lived. It says he's deceased.'

'Where do you think this comes from?' I ask. 'What tests were they doing?'

Sebastian shrugs. 'I have no idea. You're the one who wants to be a doctor one day, what do you think?' He passes the folder over to me.

I look over its contents, reading the file more thoroughly than Sebastian's cursory glance. 'It says they were trialling some sort of gene therapy,' I eventually say, 'but I don't understand half of what I'm reading, so who knows what exactly they were doing.' I pass the folder back to Sebastian, not wanting to look at the picture of the dead man's face any longer.

Sebastian continues reading over it. 'Look at the date. The file is from ten years ago. This guy's long gone,' he says.

I shudder and walk over to another one of the covered shapes in the room. It's much larger than the others and I feel curious about what's underneath the sheet, but also cautious.

I trail my fingers along the face of the white sheet, listening to Sebastian as he continues to talk about the man in the file.

'Under his results it just says 'Level 2'. What do you think that means?'

I shrug. 'No idea.'

'It's got to mean something,' he mutters under his breath. He's quiet as he continues reading.

I bend down to carefully lift up one corner of the sheet. Pulling it up, I find a glass cabinet that houses a series of vases. I tug my sleeve down over my hand and wipe the thin coat of dust from the glass. Using the small light from my CommuCuff, I can clearly make out words inscribed into the small bronze tag that labels the first urn. 'In Remembrance,' is engraved on the first line followed by a name and two dates...

I gasp and quickly drop the sheet back down.

'You alright?' Sebastian asks.

'Yes.' I stumble backwards, accidently bumping into a chair as I manoeuvre away from the cabinet. 'Yes, I'm fine.'

'Should we see what else is up here?' Sebastian asks, tossing the folder back on the table.

I glance back towards the cabinet. 'Yeah, let's go. This room gives me the creeps.'

We move out into the hallway, which is also dark and completely deserted. I don't know what I expected to find, but it appears as if no one's been here in a long time. The emptiness is eerie and the thought of the urns filled with people's remains, abandoned up here long ago, makes the hairs on the back of my neck stand on end.

'Does anyone even come up here anymore?' I ask, instinctively whispering in the abandoned hallway.

Sebastian opens the door to another room only to find more covered furniture. 'Doesn't look like it,' he says as he closes the door and we continue down the hallway.

'Why would they bother to seal these levels off if there isn't anything here?' he wonders aloud.

I open the next door we come across, expecting to see more of the same. 'I wouldn't speak so soon,' I murmur.

The doorway leads to another hallway, but it's clear even in the dark, that this one is lined with cells.

Sebastian shines his torch through the clear glass wall of the first cell, then into the second. 'Are you thinking the same thing I am?' he asks, turning the torch onto a third.

'They've got hospital beds in them, and life support equipment. Do you think this is where...' I can barely finish the sentence. It's quite obvious this is where they brought the tainted. They were sick and needed help, but I guess they also needed restraint.

'So why aren't they still here?' Sebastian asks, distress creeping into his voice.

The question I'm more concerned with is: what did they do to them? My stomach drops as I think about the urns again.

'I don't know,' I respond softly. 'Maybe we'll find something in one of the other rooms?'

Sebastian nods sadly and I take his hand, guiding him back out to the main hallway. He's quiet as we continue checking out the other rooms and I can tell he's worrying about his family. There's nothing I can say though to make it any better. I don't know anymore than he does about where they've gone.

'Do you think they're dead?' Sebastian asks when we turn down yet another abandoned hallway. The question shocks me and there's no easy way to respond.

'You know I think they're still alive,' I say simply. 'Just because we haven't found them up here doesn't mean they're dead.'

'Yeah I know. I really thought we might find them here is all.' Sebastian falls silent again, and I leave him to his thoughts.

We reach a door at the end of the hallway that's locked. Sebastian puts his shoulder into it as he tries to shove it open, but the door stays firmly shut. After several more failed attempts he steps back and runs his torch light along the doorway, as though searching for another way through. The light catches on a shiny biometric security panel and I realise our search is at an end.

'It's no use,' I say, gently placing my hand on his back. 'There's no getting past one of those, unless whoever helped you with the Council Chambers can do it again?'

'No. They can't,' Sebastian responds flatly, before shaking my hand off his shoulder. He slowly paces away and then throws his torch down on the ground swearing. 'I really thought I'd find them up here,' he growls. 'I thought I was finally close!'

'We tried our best,' I say quietly.

'Well it's obviously not good enough.' He bends down to retrieve his torch, which thankfully survived the fall. 'How can I protect the ones I love when I don't even know what I'm up against?'

I can feel my heart breaking for him as he says this. 'No one expects you to stop them from being taken.'

'I realise that Elle, but it doesn't change the fact that all I ever wanted to do was to keep my family safe and I've quite obviously failed.'

They've been gone for such a long time I'm surprised to hear him only telling me this now. Sebastian turns and begins to walk back the way we came.

'Maybe they're in a different area up here? That door there is locked for a reason. They could be right behind it,' I say, catching up with him.

Sebastian shakes his head. 'I don't think so. Think about it, when was the last time you actually saw people walking along the top Atrium walkways?'

I try to remember and quickly realise he's right, I haven't seen anyone in years. There were never many people to walk along them in the first place, and the few I did see were back when we were kids. I'd assumed the reason for their absence was bad timing. I hadn't realised it had been years though.

'This place is totally abandoned and obviously has been for a while. It's clear there was a time when they kept the tainted up here and they're not here anymore. They've either been moved somewhere else, or they're dead,' he says bluntly.

I open my mouth to argue with him, but then close it when no words come to me. He's right; the tainted aren't here anymore. They're somewhere else or they're dead.

CHAPTER TWELVE

The next day at school I can't stop thinking about last night's exploration with Sebastian. I feel haunted by the experience and my thoughts are constantly drawn to what's happened to the tainted. It's beginning to seem more important we find out.

For so many years I assumed they were simply in another section of the ARC. It's becoming clearer though, they're nowhere close anymore and those empty cells we found only lead me to believe the worst. Just thinking they may be dead makes me feel queasy. It's enough to make me completely lose my appetite.

At lunch, I notice Gemma's eyes flicker down several times to the full bowl of food in front of me. Thankfully she doesn't ask me why I've barely eaten anything, because I have no idea what I'd tell her. She's completely focused on the dance and spends most of the break coming up with absurd ideas on how to get a good outfit.

I'm too distracted to point out the many obvious flaws in her plans. She should know setting off a fire alarm probably isn't going to help the situation. Instead I give a brief yes or no in response to each of her ideas—it's mostly no.

My eyes focus on the doorway to the cafeteria and the students streaming in and out. I haven't seen Sebastian all day and I'm concerned about him. He's so sad at the moment and I don't know how to make it better. There's also a small part of me that worries there was more to his friendship with Chelsea than he's letting on, but I try not to focus on that.

I glance over at Gemma, who is now contemplating bribing the costume room lady. I wonder what she thinks of what we overheard yesterday. Does she also think there was more to Sebastian and Chelsea's friendship than he's told me?

I want to talk about it with her, but something holds me back. Would she see me as a concerned friend or would she notice my concern is something more? I push the thought away, unwilling to admit, even to myself, that I worry more than I should.

The rest of the school day drags and teachers constantly pull me up for having my head in the clouds. It's a relief when the final bell rings and I'm dismissed for the day.

I feel a rush of excitement as I walk out of the science lab and, for the first time today, the tainted are the furthest thing from my mind. Time for the simple, yet effective, plan Gemma came up with at lunch to kick in: run like crazy to the costume room, using brute force to elbow past others if necessary.

Most of the students seem to be massing towards the costume room, so I have to duck and weave to get past them. I didn't want to resort to using my elbows but I find I need them, if only for self-defence. If there's one thing a school dance teaches you, it's that clothing brings out the worst in girls—and some boys.

When I make it to the costume room I'm pretty pleased with myself. There's barely anyone here yet and I've managed to get reasonably close to the front of the line. I should definitely be able to pick up something decent from here. Unfortunately, Gemma is nowhere to be seen.

The line moves forward quickly and after only a few minutes of waiting I find myself walking into the costume room. Although, given the size of the room and its contents, 'closet' is probably a more appropriate description. The room is packed with clothing from before impact, with colourful dresses and material bulging from the clothes racks. There's barely enough room to walk between the rows.

They have a one person in, one person out policy, and the girl walking out as I go in has the biggest grin on her face, which is promising. I must be early enough to get something good.

As I enter I am bombarded by the riot of colour inside and my greys seem even more dull and lifeless than usual. I squeeze my way between two racks of dresses to begin my hunt for the perfect dress. On the first rack I try the clothes are pretty old and really beginning to show their age. I quickly skip to a different clothes rack. You have to be ruthless, yet thorough, if you expect to find a hidden gem.

I'm trying to make my way through a rack of rayon, satin and taffeta, when I catch a glimpse of emerald green silk further up the rack. I walk over to it and pull out a truly beautiful dress. It has a plunging neckline with thin spaghetti straps and soft material that luxuriously drapes down to the knees.

'Perfect!' I whisper to myself.

My excitement is short lived though as I am unceremoniously thrown forward by a girl who knocks past me. The room is becoming chaotic. Girls are quickly dragging hangers across racks, eyeing off other girls' finds and shoving each other out of the way in their desperation to find an outfit. I stand up on my tiptoes and scan around. No Gemma. I carefully drape my dress over my arm and set about finding another dress for her.

Three racks later I manage to track down something suitable. It's not amazing, but I'm pretty sure at this stage it's the best I'll be able to do. I walk back towards the door and place the garments on the counter.

'That green dress is beautiful!' the teacher behind the counter says kindly. 'Oh, but I see you have another. I'm sorry but you're only allowed to take one.'

'I know. But the other is for my friend. Please, I don't know where she is and I really want her to have something nice.'

The teacher shakes her head. 'I'm sorry, I can't let you have it. It wouldn't be fair to the other students who lined up and got here early. Besides, your cuff won't let you scan out two dresses. One dress per cuff.'

Disappointed, I push the second dress towards the woman and bump my cuff roughly against the CommuSensor. With just the green dress draped over my arm I leave.

A long line winds its way from the costume room door, down the hall and around the corner. Gemma's nowhere to be seen. I try to comm her, but she doesn't answer. Then, as I make my way out of school, I stop by the library just in case she received detention. After several unsuccessful laps of the place I give up and head for the dining hall. What is she doing?

THE DINING HALL is practically deserted when I arrive. They've only just started serving dinner, so it's still quite early. There are only about ten people in here so it's a nice surprise when I notice Quinn's light blonde hair across the room. I hadn't expected to see her and it feels like ages since we've spent any time together.

'Look at what I'll be wearing to the dance tomorrow!' I say, showing Quinn the satin green dress as I approach.

'Wow,' she replies. 'That's going to look amazing! Can't say I remember seeing that one before. Maybe it's a new donation?'

'Who knows?' I respond. 'I'm just going to go get some food. Save me a seat?' I place the dress carefully over the back of the chair next to her. Quinn answers by picking her bag off the floor and dumping it firmly on the seat.

'This chair's going nowhere,' she grins up at me.

As I make my way back to my seat, with a disappointingly small serving of potato chips, I see Gemma walking in. Her shoulders are slouched and her head is slumped over. In her arms she carries some material screwed up in a tight ball.

'Mmm, chips!' Quinn exclaims when I place my tray down on the table. As quick as lightning her hand flicks to the bowl of hot chips and steals one, popping it lightly in her mouth.

'Hey!' I complain. My objection is cut off though as Gemma slumps down into the chair opposite with a groan.

'Where were you this afternoon?' I ask, slapping Quinn's hand away as she tries for another chip.

Gemma sighs and unravels the dress she has in her arms. It's pretty much a sack. A purple sack with a few choice stains across the front of it. You could definitely see how it ended up getting donated to the school.

Gemma screws it up and dumps it on the table. 'I'm in so much trouble,' she moans. 'I've been skipping some of my community service hours. I hadn't realised quite how many though. I'm down by *a lot*.'

'How many?' I ask quietly.

'*Too* many apparently. They've restricted my cuff to only emergency transmissions, they've taken away my free time credits, and according to the official they brought in to discipline me, I'll be lucky to be a janitor when I receive my apprenticeship.'

'The only positive is I still get to go to the dance on Saturday, but that's hardly a good thing when this was the only dress I could find to wear.' She pushes the purple dress aside on the table and places her head down in her hands.

I pull the beautiful dress I'd managed to find off the back of my chair. I caress its silky, supple texture in my hands and then look back at 'the sack' lying crumpled on the table. I know what I have to do.

'Here,' I offer the dress out to Gemma. 'You should have this.'

She lifts her face up from her hands to look at the beautiful green silk I'm offering her.

'Elle, I couldn't,' she whispers.

'No. You should take it,' I reply firmly. 'I said we'd get you an awesome dress for the dance, and I'm not taking no for an answer!'

She still looks uncertain.

'Besides,' I continue. 'The green will look way better on you anyways.'

'Elle!' she whispers astonished, her eyes bright with excitement. 'What would I do without you?' She jumps up from the table and runs around to hug me.

Well for starters you'd be looking like a joke at the dance, I think to myself. But then stop as I realise, the joke would now be on me.

CHAPTER THIRTEEN

No matter what I do I can't make 'the sack' look any good. It's hopeless!

To make matters worse, I still haven't talked to Sebastian since the other night and I continue to worry about him. He was so despondent and barely said two words to me as we made our way back home.

Hopefully I'll see him at the dance tonight. I catch a reflection of 'the sack' in the mirror. Then again, maybe I won't be going at all!

I'm starting to consider just wearing the usual greys tonight when Quinn comes through the door. Upon seeing me she bursts out in a fit of laughter.

She's literally crippled with it. Every time she goes to say something, it seems to hit her again even harder. I can feel my cheeks flushing bright pink with embarrassment.

'Definitely wearing the greys,' I mutter, walking across to my drawers to pull them out. Quinn manages to get a hold of herself and comes over.

'No, stop,' she says, plucking the greys out of my hand and placing them back into the drawer.

She turns and pulls an old, battered suitcase out from under her bed. Handling it ever so delicately she places it on her mattress. Her hands seem hesitant as she slowly unzips the case, and she blows out one long breath before she pushes it open.

Inside there is an explosion of colour, like the sun has crash landed on Quinn's bed and blown up in our room.

Dresses!

'You were so kind giving Gemma that dress, I think it's only fair I do the same for you,' she says.

I am speechless.

'But how?' I eventually stammer.

'My mum,' she says softly, as she turns around and sits. 'I don't know if I ever really told you, but I wasn't like you—you know, orphaned from the start. I came to the ARC with my mum.' Her eyes glaze over and seem to stare beyond the bedroom wall.

'I was seven at the time, so I can remember the trip quite well. Mum had been chosen to come here prior to the asteroid hitting.' A hint of pride edges on her voice as she says this, but her face quickly drops and she frowns.

'It was near impossible for us to leave though. My dad had cancer and was close to dying. They wouldn't let him come. Bastards said they didn't have room for someone who was just going to die anyway. Mum didn't want to leave him, she wanted to stay with him to the end, but she came to save me. Only three years later she was taken.'

'I had no idea,' I say, unsure of how to comfort her. For as long as I've known Quinn, I've wondered about her past. She has always had a tendency to immediately shrug off any questions or only respond with short, vague answers.

'Well, it's not really the type of thing I enjoy talking about. I guess that's why I've never really brought it up.' She pauses, and I stand watching her in silence.

She looks uncomfortable after sharing the burden she carries. Quinn's never been big on delving into feelings that upset or trouble her. A moment later her face completely transforms, masking any pain she feels. 'So back to the dress!' she says perkily, effectively closing shut the door she'd briefly opened to her past.

'Here.' She offers out a beautiful pastel lemon dress. It is strapless, with a tight silk bustier and a sheer, chiffon skirt that poofs out from the waist. 'You'll look like the most beautiful ray of sunshine in this one,' she says, handing it to me. 'But you better believe I will hunt you down if you so much as think of getting it dirty! I know where you live!'

I hold it in my hands, not quite able to believe this is happening.

'Did you ever read that children's story, Cinderella?' I ask. 'Because I'm pretty certain you're my fairy godmother.'

'Hmm, well I don't think Cinderella was issued with death threats, but I'll take it.'

I practically tear 'the sack' off my body, feeling relieved to be rid of it forever. I put on Quinn's dress and give a spin before asking how I look.

'Like I said, a ray of sunshine!' she responds.

As I WALK to the sports centre, where the dance is being held, for one of the few times in my life I feel truly special. Quinn had spent over an hour fixing my hair, and applying some of her precious makeup. When I had seen myself in the mirror it had taken me a minute to recognize myself looking back out of it. The dark, smoky eye shadow Quinn had applied made my blue eyes pop, the soft pink lipstick gave me positively luscious lips, and my hair fell in soft waves, similar to Quinn's.

I almost feel beautiful.

Arriving at the dance, I'm nervous. I've never really cared what other people think of how I look, but now I stupidly feel the need for their approval. My stomach flutters as I wonder what Sebastian will think. I quickly adjust my dress to make sure it sits just right, then pull my shoulders back and walk in.

The basketball courts have been converted for the occasion. The battered old disco ball they always bring out hangs over the dance floor and an array of coloured lights flash as they dance around the room. A long stage has been set up in front of one of the basketball hoops and some of the boys from school, who have a rock band called 'Taken Nation,' play on top of it. The room is packed with people, all dressed in clothes from before.

I spot Gemma chatting with a group of girls. They are gushing over how amazing she looks in the green dress. I feel so happy watching her show it off. Especially after how horrible her last dance experience had been. 'The sack' was practically haute couture compared with the last outfit she had worn. She had been completely embarrassed by the whole ordeal. I wouldn't be surprised if she still had nightmares over it.

I am standing watching from just inside the doorway when I feel someone come up behind me. A deep male voice whispers in my ear.

'You look amazing.'

The voice makes me jump. 'Sebastian...' I laugh at my reaction and turn.

'Ryan?' I ask, startled. 'I thought... W-What are you doing here?' My eyes dart over to the crowd on the dance floor. Is anyone watching? I notice an official standing over by the drinks table looking in this direction, and it puts me on edge. I feel too exposed standing out here with him, so before he can answer I pull him by his sleeve out of the sports centre and into one of the nearby classrooms. I close the door firmly behind me. He goes and sits on the teacher's desk while I stride over to stand in front of him.

'Seriously, what are you doing here?' I ask again. It's such strange behaviour for him to come see me at a school dance. I wouldn't want people to get the wrong idea.

'I don't know,' he says confused. 'I'm not supposed to be here,' he mutters.

'Then what are you doing here? A few days ago you said I wouldn't be seeing you for a while.'

'A few days ago,' he repeats. He seems really addled.

'Yes ... in the Plantation,' I expand.

'The Plantation... Yes, you're right. We won't be seeing each other for a while.' I shake my hands at him as his says this. Won't see him for a while? I'm seeing him right now.

'Oh yeah, well besides tonight of course,' he mutters. 'I didn't realise I would get to see you tonight.'

'Didn't realise?' I ask. 'But *you* came to *my* school dance. How do you not realise you're going to see me when you do that?'

His face closes up and I come to the conclusion I'm not getting any answers tonight.

'Listen Elle, I don't want to get into any of that,' he says in his no-nonsense voice. Then his expression softens. 'I'm just glad I get to see you tonight. You are so incredibly beautiful.'

He stands up from leaning against the teacher's desk, steps towards me and lightly cups my shoulders in his hands.

'So beautiful,' he whispers again. He moves himself closer and lightly kisses my forehead. I can't move. I am overwhelmed by his sweet, masculine smell that surrounds me. I feel completely lightheaded.

All too quickly he steps away from me.

'Well, we can't have Cinderella missing the ball,' he says lightly.

I laugh awkwardly. Tonight really does seem like the night for fairy tales. I look at him and all I can think is if he comes that close again I'd quite happily miss the ball. As quickly as the thought enters my head I dismiss it. *What am I thinking?*

Instead I say, 'No. Well Prince Charming is probably inside waiting for me.' For just a second I see a frown cross his face, but it is gone so quickly I have to wonder if I imagined it.

'You should go,' he says, nodding his head toward the door.

'Right,' I respond. I walk over to the door and turn back one last time.

'Have a good night,' he says, as I pull my eyes away from his.

When I make my entrance for a second time, I no longer feel nervous. Confused is probably a more appropriate term. What was with Ryan tonight? I spot Gemma dancing in the crowd and make my way over to her.

'Elle!' She practically squeals upon seeing me. With complete unabashed enthusiasm she runs over and throws her arms around me. Then, with one swift movement she stands back to give me an obvious once over.

'You. Look. Amazing!' she gushes, her voice even louder and more high-pitched than before.

'You look better!' I call back, attempting to be heard over the music.

'No sack?' she asks.

'No sack!' I reply. 'I'll tell you about it later. Are you having fun?'

'So much fun!' she exclaims. 'And who knew there were so many cute boys in our year. They really scrub up okay, don't they?'

I have to admit, she's right. It definitely seems like the boys in our year at school have grown up. I notice several of them are looking at Gemma.

'I think they think you scrub up okay yourself!' I say. She looks around nervously, but I can tell she's excited to hear it. I guess Cam has some competition.

'C'mon, let's go dance.' She grabs my hand and pulls me through the crowd and into the thick of it.

I have to admit the dance is awesome. We jump around and sing along to all the songs, even though we don't know the words. I look like an idiot, convulsing around the dance floor, but I'm having too much fun to care. For the first time in ages I feel like I'm finally letting loose.

I notice Cam dancing just behind Gemma. He looks like he's trying to catch her attention with some ludicrous dance moves, but she's completely oblivious he's there. I yell to Gemma over the music, 'I'm getting a drink.'

'Come back soon,' she shouts back.

I head towards Cam as I try to move through the crowd towards the drinks table. When I get to him I stand on my tiptoes to get close to his ear. 'Just ask her to dance already!' I yell loudly.

'Okay,' he yells back. 'Only if you promise not to tell her about the moves I was just pulling!'

'I think it's better no one knows about those.'

He laughs and begins to slowly dance-shuffle his way over to Gemma. Within minutes they're dancing together and I think it's safe to say she's forgotten how cute the other boys are looking tonight.

It's a relief to get out from inside the crowd. I head over to the drinks table and finish off several glasses of water. Everyone is having such a good night. Even Kate walks past me and doesn't have a bad word to say.

I place my glass down on the table and turn to see Sebastian edging along the drinks table to stand rigidly beside me. He's wearing a black tailored suit that fits him remarkably well. His hair is gelled back and he is strangely at ease in the foreign outfit. He looks amazing, but I would never admit that aloud.

'Hey,' he says distantly. His eyes look at me darkly and he's frowning as though he's angry. I don't understand why. We stand in silence for a minute as I wait for him to explain.

'Is everything okay?' I ask him, when he continues to stand there glaring at me.

All he will say though is, 'I need to speak with you.'

'What's up?' I ask. He jerks his head towards the exit and motions for me to follow him. I'm not certain why he's acting this way, so I follow him quietly.

The music is loud and everyone in the room is happy, but as we walk over to the doors and out the exit I feel like we're in our own quiet bubble of tension, and everything outside of it is muted. Sebastian hunches over as he walks and I can practically see the unease radiating off him.

There are several couples making out in the hallway, in seriously overt sessions of PDA. I wish we could laugh about them together, as we usually would, but Sebastian ignores them completely. He walks straight by them, oblivious, as he heads over to the same classroom I had been in with Ryan just a few hours ago.

He marches into the room ahead of me, stops in the middle and continues to face away from me.

'What do you want to talk about?' I ask, attempting to sound as neutral as possible.

'I saw you,' he says, turning to look at me.

'What do you mean?'

'I saw you with *him* earlier.'

'Who, Ryan?' I ask, confused.

'Yes,' he says, through his teeth, his eyes narrowing at me.

'And...'

'God Elle,' he groans. 'Don't you get it?' He turns and paces up and down in front of me. 'You're just ... well ... you're dating someone who is completely wrong for you,' he hurls at me.

'What?' Of all the things Sebastian could have said to me I didn't expect that. As I think through the implications of what he's saying I begin to worry. Does he really think Ryan and I are together? Surely he knows there's nothing between us.

'*We're* not dating,' I finally say. My voice is thick with accusation. He's been the one hiding a relationship, not me. I clench my jaw shut and turn away from him. I take slow, deep breaths and try to quell the wild arguments that run rampant through my mind. I don't want to fight with him.

He doesn't respond to what I've said and his lack of words make me worry him and Chelsea actually were together. My stomach lurches at the thought. I ignore the sudden empty sensation inside and try to suppress my feelings. 'I'm sorry. I don't want to fight Sebastian. I just want to be your friend, especially when you're hurting like this. I'm so sorry your girlfriend was taken.'

'Girlfriend?' he asks, confused. 'What gave you the impression Chelsea was my girlfriend?'

'I overheard some guys talking and then when you took me up to the top levels the other night it kind of confirmed it. It's okay, I'm not mad you didn't tell me.'

'Well of course I didn't tell you. It's not true! I mean, don't get me wrong, Chelsea and I are friends and we used to hang out, but nothing more. Since when did you listen to gossip over me?' he asks.

I shrug off his question. 'Girlfriend or not though, I know you must be sad.'

'Don't worry about it Elle. I'm fine,' he reassures me.

He takes a step towards me. His eyes look into mine deeply as he says, 'Besides, don't you know, there's only one girl for me.' I feel my heart leap inside of me.

'You said you weren't dating him?' he asks, moving closer.

'No,' I respond. 'I mean, I see him around, he kind of just turns up, but we never *do* anything. I think he just likes to see how I am.' I'm rambling as I try to work out how this conversation turned a corner so quickly.

'Really?' he says, stepping so close that I can almost feel the heat from his body. I take an involuntary step back and bump against a desk.

'Yes really. What's it to you anyways?' I ask.

'Well,' he says, taking a final step to close the distance I've put between us. 'It suits my interests for you to not be with him.'

'I don't know what you're talking about,' I say. I try not to look at him, but he's so close now that I don't have too many options. I end up just staring at his chest.

'You said you didn't kiss me during spin the bottle because you don't want to ruin our friendship.'

I nod, feeling confused and wishing he hadn't brought *that* up again.

'Surely you must know that no matter what, we will always be friends.'

'I guess,' I mumble.

'I've been thinking a lot these last few days, and one thing I've realised is that there may not be a tomorrow, so we've got to live for today. I realised if I only had one day left then I would want you to know the truth.'

'What truth?' I barely whisper the words.

He gently takes my hand in his. 'Elle, if you're going to be with anyone, it's meant to be me.' He looks down into my eyes, searching for my answer.

'You are so beautiful tonight,' he says tenderly.

I close my eyes and smile at his words, feeling lighter and happier than I can ever remember. When I open my eyes again to look up at him he's watching me and there's a powerful desire in his eyes that I can feel awaken something inside of me.

Ever so slowly he puts his hands on my waist and begins to lower his head towards mine. I swallow, feeling nervous because I know this is the moment we're going to kiss. My blood simmers beneath the surface of my skin, which seems to buzz with so much electricity that the hairs on my arms stand on end.

With unexpected courage, I place my hands on his arms and then slowly allow them to make their way up to his neck. He shivers as my fingers trace along his skin, leaving a wake of goose bumps along his arms. He grips the back of my waist tighter, drawing me closer to him. Our faces are now only inches apart and I can feel his warm breath against my lips. He takes a moment and then ever so gently he brushes his lips against mine.

They are as light as a feather being traced along my lips and I feel a thrilling jolt of electricity pass through my body. I long for more, but the door swings open, hitting the wall with a bang.

We both jump and Sebastian turns to look at the door. I quickly look down at his chest, feeling breathless, like I've just run a half marathon.

'Oh sorry,' some guy drawls from inside the doorway, a girl hanging off of his arm. 'Didn't realise this room was taken.' He lurches back out, dragging the girl with him and leaving the door ajar.

Sebastian still holds me in his arms, but the moment has gone, and I don't quite know what to do. We stand frozen for a few seconds before he slides his hands from my waist and steps back. It's only one step, but it feels like he's a mile away.

I touch my fingers against my lips, trying to stop them from trembling along with the rest of my body. I can't manage to bring myself to look Sebastian in the eye.

'Are you okay?' he asks.

I nod, not trusting myself to speak. He goes to take my hand in his, but I shy away.

'What's wrong?'

I shake my head.

'Elle, please talk to me. Did you not want this?' I can hear the fear clearly in his voice, the worry that I regret what just happened.

'No,' the word catches in my throat and I clear it. 'No, of course I did ... but we can't.'

'Why not?'

'I can't get close to you. I can't risk it when I could so easily lose you.'

He grasps my hand firmly in his and looks me in the eyes. 'Elle. I'm not going anywhere and whether or not I kiss you isn't going to change how I feel. Can you really imagine feeling closer to me than you already do?'

I pull my hand from his. 'Yes,' I whisper quietly. I know beyond a shadow of a doubt that opening my heart to him would be the worst kind of mistake. That if I gave into him, dared to love him, and he left, I would be shattered and would never recover.

I push my feelings down and lock them away. No matter how much I want to be with him, I know that staying friends is for the best. 'This,' I wave my hand between the two of us, 'was an accident. Some sort of school dance ... accident.'

'No,' he replies quietly.

'Please?' I plead with him.

He steps back from me, hurt evident on his face. My hands lift unconsciously in response. I want to reach out to him. I want to take his hands in mine again, to feel the tingles that flutter inside me at his touch. I want to tell him he's all I've ever wanted and I would risk anything to be with him, but I've lost too much and I can't bring myself to open up to him the way I desperately want to.

I force my hands back down to my side. 'We're fine. Let's just pretend this never happened. Goodnight Sebastian.' I turn away, not waiting for him to respond and walk out the open door.

CHAPTER FOURTEEN

I punch my pillow, trying to make it sit just right, roll onto my back and face the ceiling. I haven't seen Sebastian since the dance and it's been three whole days.

He's tried to comm me several times since then, but the comms have stopped coming now and I know he must be avoiding me. Then again, I've probably been avoiding him as well. I know I should go and visit him or at least comm him back, but I don't feel ready to face him just yet. We'd left things so awkwardly at the dance.

We barely even kissed and it was enough to change everything. It's awakened something inside of me, something I know I shouldn't want. Him.

I'm interrupted from my unsettling thoughts as Quinn enters our room and dumps her bag onto the table.

'Hey,' she says, as she walks over and collapses down on her bed. She groans tiredly and stretches out on it.

'Tough day?' I ask.

'Yeah. We had a problem with one of the storage rooms, but it's all fixed now.' She rolls towards me and props herself up on her elbow.

'Are you still moping about Sebastian?' she asks. 'Oh I can never keep up!'

'Very funny,' I respond. I haven't even told her what happened at the dance and she's pretty much hit the nail on the head. It's unbelievable how intuitive she can be sometimes.

'And no,' I lie. 'I guess I'm just concerned about that girl that was taken last week, Chelsea.' This at least is partially true.

Quinn's face softens. 'I know it can be difficult. Especially when you know the person. How about we go and take your mind off things. Do you want to go see a movie? I hear they're showing some classics tonight.'

A movie is probably the last thing I want right now, but somehow the words, 'yeah that sounds great,' tumble out of my mouth. I guess she's right. I could really use the distraction.

THERE's a large group of people waiting by the entrance to the cinema room when we arrive. Quinn's instantly beckoned over by a group of guys she knows. I tell her to go over without me, I'm really not in the mood for small talk, but she drags me along anyway.

I can't be bothered interacting with them and it's pretty obvious they have about as much interest in me as I have in talking to them. Boys generally are indifferent to me when Quinn's around, except for maybe Sebastian. Who knows if that's changed now? My thoughts flicker to the time we'd seen Ryan here. Maybe not *all* guys are so indifferent.

We'd been standing out the front of the cinema, much the same as we are doing now when I had seen him.

'Quinn, Quinn!' I had exclaimed tugging on her sleeve. 'It's *him*. The guy I saw at breakfast a few weeks ago.'

'Where?' she responded, looking inquisitively at all the guys surrounding us.

'There, with the dark hair, the tall one standing by the—'

'I see him,' she said, cutting me off. 'Oh he's hot! But definitely way too old for you! Let's go say hi!'

Before I had a chance to respond she just grabbed my hand and dragged me over to him.

'Hi I'm Quinn,' she sparkled at him. He looked down at us. Well I shouldn't say us; really he had just looked at me.

'Hi Quinn,' he said, still looking at me. 'Hi Elle.' His voice almost caressed my name. I was so captivated, I didn't even realise he knew my name.

All I managed was to squeak out a, 'hi,' in response. Quinn had already moved into attack mode and was oozing on the charm in a way only she could get away with. I don't remember what she was saying at the time. All I remember was the way he looked at me; *that* he was looking at me.

He turned from me and looked up at the cinema room door.

'Girls if you want to see Breakfast at Tiffany's I suggest you get a move on.'

We had both been quick to turn and head towards the open doors. I turned to say goodbye but found him nowhere to be seen.

'Hey Elle, anyone home?' Cam says, waking me from my daydream. My eyes refocus from the spot on the far wall I'd been absorbed with while thinking, to find him standing in front of me, with that annoying self-assured smirk of his.

'Hey Cam, how's it going?'

'Yeah, good. I had my testing today.' He shows his arm and the little red mark on it. 'Took it like a real champ though, didn't I.'

'Good to see someone who wears their needle jab with such glory,' I say laughing.

'Yeah well it's a good sign, isn't it. Have to admit, it's the first one I haven't been nervous about. With Chelsea being taken last week, I was pretty sure my chances were low.'

'I don't think that really makes a difference,' I suggest.

'Oh well, I survived. That's the main thing eh?' I nod in agreement. There's no denying the relief you feel coming back from your testing; knowing you're safe for another year.

'Hey, do you know if Sebastian's feeling any better?' he asks.

'Any better?' I say, confused.

'I figured he was sick, considering he's been off from school the last two days.'

'No sorry, I had no idea.' *Shit.* He must really want to avoid me.

'Elle,' Quinn taps me on the shoulder. 'The movie's starting.' She points over at the door and the people walking in.

'Well enjoy the movie,' I say to Cam.

'Yeah, you too.'

I walk in with Quinn and find seats that are nice and close to the screen. From what Quinn had said the movie was a comedy, and it's meant to be hilarious. I sit there waiting for the opening credits to roll, but I'm exhausted. Tired from worrying about the taking, and definitely tired of worrying about Sebastian. I'm so tired of it all, that in this warm and dark room I slowly drift away and find myself asleep.

When I open my eyes I'm on a beach. I'm lying on a towel, the sun warming my skin. I can hear the waves gently lapping at the shore. It's peaceful. Some part of my subconscious is aware I am dreaming, but I merely close my eyes and relish in the sensation. I wriggle my feet in the sand and the small grains sift around and between my toes.

It feels like I lie there for an age, cocooned in the sun's glowing warmth. Slowly I can hear the wind pick up, and the small grains of sand bite into my skin as they whisk across the empty shore.

I sit up and dust off my arms. I can see the sun slowly setting in the distance. It is not the beautiful, picturesque sunset I saw in class. Instead the sun is angry and violent. With streaks of deep red and burnt orange, it looks to claw at the surrounding sky, raging against the powers that force it to dip below the horizon. Eventually it disappears and a grey gloom resides.

It's cold. The wind picks up further. It blows away the waves and the sand. It gradually builds to the point that it batters so harshly against my body that I have to cover my head with my arms.

Abruptly, the assault stops and an eerie quiet takes over. The silence is haunting and it takes me several moments to build up the courage to open my eyes. As I peer up through my tangle of arms and hair I can see I am no longer at the beach, but surrounded by the wastelands I have so often seen projected on the Atrium screens.

I slowly stand to take in my surroundings. Dark, ominous clouds gather overhead. They roll and mushroom above like they are fighting for control of the grey and purple sky. Below the tumultuous heavens, the ground is dead and barren. The field of ice and dirt surrounds me and my bare feet freeze upon the dusty white and charcoal ground. In the distance I can make out a dead and blackened tree, a powerful contrast against this bare grey and white expanse.

I look down and find myself in a long black dress. The fabric shimmers and I put my hand down to touch it. It is soft and luxurious in my hands. As I stand admiring it I hear footsteps behind me. I turn around to find Sebastian standing there wearing his formal suit. He seems almost a part of the landscape, matching the dark colours of the ravaged earth. With one swift movement, he takes his jacket off and puts it over my shoulders. His strong, steady hands lift my chin up to look him in the eyes.

'If they took you from me, I would come for you,' he says simply.

I JERK AWAKE WITH A LOUD, raspy intake of breath. It's dark in the cinema and the people around me are laughing at one of the movie's gags.

'I've got to go,' I tell Quinn, before quickly standing to make my way to the exit, profusely apologising to the people in my row as I clamber past them.

'Where are you going?' Quinn asks, following me.

'I need to see Sebastian,' I reply, as I open the door and walk out into the bright entrance. 'We kind of had a falling out the other night and I need to make it right.'

'Well, the movie sucks anyway, let's go!' Quinn says.

I look at her surprised and begin to feel awkward. I don't know how to explain to her that I really don't want her here for this.

'Don't stress,' she says, seeing my apprehension. 'I'm going to catch up with one of the boys who lives a few doors down from Sebastian. Unless of course you want me to hold your hand?'

'Come on.' I ignore her sarcasm and tug at her sleeve so she'll follow.

WHEN WE ARRIVE out front of Sebastian's I say goodbye to Quinn, who continues on down the hallway, a cheeky smile on her face.

I take several deep breaths before I knock, three distinct raps against the door. *Knock, knock, knock,* they drum against the hollow wood.

Blood begins to churn through my body at a rapid pace as I fret over what I will say once that silver door handle turns and the door opens. I watch it with nervous anticipation, waiting for its tell-tale twisting movement to warn me I'm about to have to face Sebastian.

After several moments I knock again impatiently. Each short, staccato beat of my knuckles rapping creates a sharp, blunt echo over the gentle hum of the fluorescent lights in the hallway.

My pulse continues to escalate, and my nervous tension runs down to my fingers that fidget with the sleeves of my top. What if he's not answering the door because he doesn't want to talk to me?

'Sebastian?' I call out, refusing to accept he would blatantly ignore me this way. I cock my ear, listening for movement from the other side of the door, but don't hear anything from within.

I thump harder against the door, calling out louder. 'Sebastian?'

Quinn, having heard me from down the hallway, has walked back.

'Not home?' she asks.

I frown at the door irrationally, hating the solid object for refusing to budge. 'I guess not.' I shrug, disappointed, taking a step back from the door.

'Do you want to try comming him?' she asks.

I shake my head. It's not the kind of conversation I want to have over my cuff. 'No, I—' I've barely said two words in response when Sebastian's door handle rattles behind me.

I jump and turn around, striding back towards it, relief flooding through me. Sebastian's not ignoring me after all. I start fidgeting with my necklace, wishing I'd taken some time to consider what I should say.

As the door swings open my hand drops to my side, and I try to hide my disappointment. The face that greets me through the crack in the slightly ajar door is not Sebastian, but his dad.

I rush to explain to him that I'm here to see Sebastian. My voice trails off though when I look at Adam more closely. His head barely peeks out from behind the door, but it's enough to show he's devastated. His eyes are red and puffy, his skin is so white it's almost grey, and angry tears fall down his tired, drawn face.

Before I can ask him what's wrong he opens the door wide, steps forward and hugs me, his body shaking in my arms. Feeling confused, I look over his shoulder to Quinn, but she seems just as baffled.

'I'm sorry Elle. I'm so sorry,' he sobs. His voice is husky and breaking with emotion.

My heart stops beating. It refuses to continue its happy thudding, like a cold, clammy hand has wrapped its way around it and clenches it angrily in its grasp. There's only one thing Adam Scott has left to lose that could make him this distraught. Nausea builds in my stomach and my own arms quiver heavily as I stand back from him, my hands lightly clinging to his trembling shoulders.

'What's happened?' I can barely say the words. They feel thick and heavy, like trying to talk with a mouthful of dirt.

'They've... They've...' he wheezes.

'Are you okay Adam?' Quinn comes up behind him and begins rubbing his back.

'I just thought he was sick. Thought I was doing the right thing,' he splutters. I look at Quinn desperately, the bile in my stomach now sitting in my throat.

'Adam, what happened?' she asks, when she sees I can't bring myself to speak.

He looks me dead in the eyes and in this moment I know with absolute certainty I don't want to hear the words he's about to say.

'They've taken him Elle,' he cries. 'Sebastian. They've taken him. He's *tainted* and he's never coming back.'

CHAPTER FIFTEEN

As an orphan, you often wonder about your parents. Mostly it's the small things that plague you. Questions like, what perfume did my mum wear? Or what kind of music did my dad listen to? Did he even listen to music? You wonder about the little things you would know if they were with you.

Sometimes you allow yourself to go a little further. You touch on questions like, what did my parents look like? Do I have my mum's eyes or my dad's nose?

Unsurprisingly, you then make your way to a big one; did they love me? From there you inevitably have to ask the question that hurts the most. If they did love me, how could they let me go?

As I stand looking at Adam, who is still gripping my arms but has now collapsed down onto his knees, his face in total agony, my mind drifts away from my body. Reality feels like an echo, as if I'm underwater while life rages on above the surface. As my mind floats through calmer seas I wonder, how could Sebastian leave me?

I snap back to reality. Sebastian didn't leave me. He hadn't wanted to leave. He was taken.

I back away from Adam, tearing myself from the grip he has on my arms. He flops limply down onto the floor. Looking up at Quinn I can see pain on her face, but also worry. She's not worried for Sebastian, or even Adam. She's worried for me.

Her pity is a haunting emphasis of what has just happened. Sebastian is gone.

'I can't...' I utter. I turn away from her troubled stare, and Adam's crumpled body lying on the ground, and without another word I run.

I run through endless corridors not knowing where my feet will take me. When I reach the Atrium I have to slow my pace as I try to push past all the people. In my rush to get out of the suffocating crowd I fall over, my knees slamming harshly against the ground. Legs bump past me as people carelessly walk by.

'Are you okay?' A woman crouches down beside me. I can feel her hand at my elbow, attempting to help me up, but I shake her off. Without looking at the woman or thanking her I hurry on, roughly shoving my way through the multitudes.

When the crowd starts to disperse I begin to run again, faster this time. I want to get away from the people who had stared at me as I stumbled through the Atrium. Away from those who had judged me as I flew past them in the corridor. Away from everyone who doesn't understand what it's like to lose your best friend.

'Ah!' I yell out and grab my stomach in pain as it urges me to stop running with a brutal cramp. I put pressure on it and struggle on. I'm still not far enough from the thought that Sebastian's no longer here.

When I physically can't continue I finally collapse on the floor in a deserted corridor. I drag my broken body over to the wall and lean against it, defeated. I feel weak and weary and my breath is uncontrollable as I heave in and out. I pull my knees in tight to my chest and bow my head into them.

Surely this is a mistake. Surely they have taken the wrong person. Two takings in a matter of days; that just doesn't happen now.

I feel a sob tear through my chest. I should've gone to find him before tonight. Now I will never have the chance to make things right with him. He has gone where I can't follow.

I sit for what seems like hours, miserable. No one comes to find me and no one walks past. I am left in my own little world of pain.

I eventually awaken from my distraught state when I hear movement in the distance. It takes me a moment to recognise the sound of footsteps coming closer. I try to orientate myself.

Where am I?

I can vaguely remember passing the smell of manure wafting from the animal pens earlier, and looking at the wide corridor and high ceiling, I'm almost certain I'm in the East Wing. In a rush of arms and legs, I stand up, placing my hand against the wall to steady myself. I shouldn't be in here. If I'm caught loitering here without permission I'll be in trouble. Knowing my luck, I'd end up before the Council.

I start to walk away from the footsteps. I feel even more confused as I turn down another corridor. Why hadn't I paid attention earlier? I don't recognise anything.

I stop abruptly as a new sound reaches my ears from up ahead. I lower my head and tilt my ear in the direction of the sound, holding my breath for fear of missing the noise again.

There it is. My head snaps up and I look in the direction I've been walking. Male voices, coming this way. I glance back over my shoulder towards the footsteps I'd initially heard. I'm stuck in the middle.

I look up and down the hallway for somewhere to hide. There's a door a little further down, so I make a dash for it. I slam my hand down on the handle and shove my body against it.

It's locked. *Dammit!*

I bite down on my lower lip. Codes, codes. Umm. One, two, three, four? I punch the code into the keypad. The keypad light goes red. No luck. I try a couple of other random combinations.

'Ah, it's no use,' I mutter angrily at the keypad, jamming my hand against the numbers violently.

The voices are getting louder, and closer. They'll be here any second.

I'm about to give up and start running when the code Ryan gave me the other day for the Plantation pops into my head. Surely not... What were those numbers again? Four, three, five and eight—no that's not right—nine...

The keypad lights up green and I burst through the door, shutting it quickly behind me.

I feel a rush of relief as the door clicks shut, me safely on the other side. I lean my head against the door to listen. The men are much closer and I can just make out some of their words. My nerves tingle in my fingers. I'm not out of the woods yet. While I wait for them to move on, I turn to see where I am.

If I thought I was confused about where I was before, it's nothing compared to how I feel now. I'm in a corridor that's *completely* foreign to me. Nothing is familiar. The white walls are covered with dust and dirt. The light overhead hangs uselessly from the ceiling. Thankfully the blue sensor lights that line the walkway are functioning.

I've definitely never been to this section of the ARC. Intrigued, I step away from the door and take a few steps down the corridor. It reminds me of the far corner of the North Wing, where Quinn and I live. But it's much older and completely silent. Whilst our forsaken corner is quiet, it is nothing compared to the eerie abandonment I find here.

Picking one of the doors that lead off the hallway, I slowly edge it open. The air inside is cold and stale, and my footprints leave a trail in the dust that has settled on the floor. As I push the door open further I can make out what appears to be an old and deteriorated living quarters. The white sheets on the beds are covered with dust, and the beds themselves seem to have sagged in the centre. Spider webs intricately weave long thin nets across the corners of the room.

'I'm in the Old Wing,' I murmur.

I start to feel nervous. I'm not meant to be here, like *really* not meant to be here. No one is.

The Old Wing is forbidden to everyone in the ARC. It was the first place people came when fleeing in preparation for the asteroid. The ARC had been quick to reach capacity and the Council was forced to make an order to close the entrance. The only means of effectively closing the entrance so no one could get in, or so no one could get out, was to set off some explosive material so it would implode. Unfortunately it didn't set off as planned and the implosion made the whole wing unstable.

I'm not just in trouble. I'm in danger.

I begin to follow my footprints back to the Old Wing entrance, but as I get near I can hear voices from right on the other side of it. I stop to listen.

Are they coming in here?

I cock my ear and as I do I catch the sound of a code being entered into the door. *Shit.* I turn and start running deeper into the wing. I can't be caught in here. I'll take on an unstable structure any day over a run in with officials.

I stumble and stagger over loose rubble that lies haphazardly on the ground. I don't look back, and I don't stop to listen. After a good ten minutes of jogging, turning down countless corridors and having thoroughly lost myself, I slow to a walk.

For what seems like hours I traipse through a labyrinth of old and endless hallways. I have no idea where I am and no idea how to get back home.

I am beginning to lose hope when I hear the soft sound of voices echoing through the corridor. Someone is close by. My first thought is to call out to them. I open my mouth to yell, but stop myself before any sound comes out. I may be lost but that's nothing compared to the trouble I'll be in if I'm found.

I creep towards the voices, my natural instinct for self-preservation at war with my desperate need for guidance. Someone is speaking, but I'm unable to make out what they're saying.

The voices get louder when I reach a junction with a corridor that is slightly better lit than the darkness I've been stumbling through. I can hear the shuffle and scrape of footsteps, the movement only becoming louder as I wait.

I stand slightly back from the intersection. If I turn left I'll be caught, but turning right means whoever's down here will be snapping at my heels.

Instead, I retrace my steps, shrinking back into the darkness as a ball of light, emanating from a torch, bounces on the ground near me.

I watch from the shadows of a doorway down the adjacent corridor as the first man passes. From here I can easily make out the stark white official uniform. What the hell are they doing here?

As I wait for them to pass, I try to figure out where they could be going. Then it hits me. Maybe there's a reason why the Old Wing is forbidden? It's where they take the *tainted*! It has to be.

Hope flares inside of me. I had told Sebastian I would come for him and now I can!

When the last official walks past the light gradually fades. I move into the corridor and quietly begin to follow.

They walk further and further into the Old Wing. I feel exhausted, emotionally and physically drained, but determination propels me forward.

The men stop up ahead. As they do I count their dark shadows outlined dimly in the distance. There are six of them standing in front of a large rock, which appears to block the way. One by one they disappear behind it.

As I near the rock my heart beats so fast and so loudly, it fills my ears with its constant thudding. The light the men carried has disappeared now and only the soft blue glow remains.

I find a tunnel entrance carved into the stone concealed behind the rock. There are no reliable blue lights lining this route and it appears to be one *very* small space. It's tall enough for me to walk through without ducking my head, but incredibly narrow. I wonder how the officials managed to make it through. I lean forward and try to peer further down the passage but the darkness inside is so thick I can't see more than two feet ahead.

I take deep breaths in and out. *'You can do this,'* I tell myself. I just need to take one step after another. Trying not to think about it, I make my way into the tunnel.

A few steps in and the little light I did have has completely disappeared. The pitch black is all encompassing, suffocating even. Fear stirs in my belly and I can feel my body begin to tense and stiffen. The space is even smaller than I'd first imagined. *'Don't think about it,'* I repeat to myself several times. Now is seriously not the time for a breakdown.

I quickly activate my CommuCuff, so I can at least have some light to guide me, but the light from the cuff is almost negligible. With my trembling hand held out in front I begin to make my way through the tight passage, sliding my other hand along the rough rock to steady myself. Although I'm terrified of being trapped in this dark, forsaken passage, the thought of losing Sebastian forever is much, much worse.

In some sections I find I need to turn sideways to inch my way through the tight and narrow confines. I squeeze my eyes shut, terrified, as I edge my way along with rock pressing in from all around me.

Finally the tunnel begins to widen enough so I can walk without risk of being wedged and I find the darkness also begins to lessen. Then finally, in the distance, I can make out the tiniest orb of light. I clamber my way towards it, desperate to get out of here. It quickly gets bigger and brighter, until finally I am standing at the end of the tunnel.

Very carefully, in case the officials are still around, I peer around one of the rocks to see where I've been led. As I do I have to stifle a gasp.

Before me stands a huge cavern. High above a mass of rock forms the roof. It is lined with precarious looking stalactites of all shapes and sizes that look like they could fall at any moment. Dotted among them are long electric lights, which glow just bright enough so the floor far below is lit. Right in the centre is a metal walkway that cuts the cavern in half. The officials I followed here walk along it easily chatting to each other, almost oblivious to the giant walls that tower above them. Further ahead I can see another set of officials getting up and gathering their stuff as if to leave.

It's then I see it. On the far side of the cavern, just behind where the officials sit, large boulders are piled one on top of the other, almost like an enormous landslide.

'The entrance,' I whisper to myself.

I have spent all of my life hearing about it, but I never thought I would get to see it. I feel such awe looking at the place I must have come through 15 years ago—the entranceway to our salvation.

My heart sinks though as I realise it's *completely* closed up. There's no entrance or exit here anymore. On closer inspection I can see the whole area is roped off. Not even the officials go over the other side of the rope. It must be unstable. The officials are guarding it, protecting it and us.

I also realise there are no citizens with the officials, let alone any of the tainted. I watch for a while longer, but when I don't see anything more to support my wild theory, I miserably decide it's time to go home. As I turn back to the tunnel a figure steps out from the shadows.

My whole body seizes up and I freeze as a man dressed in the white uniform of an official materialises before me. There's nowhere for me to run and nowhere for me to hide. I doubt there are any words I'll be able to use to get myself out of this one.

I slowly look up to the man's face, expecting the worst, and gasp.

'Elle?' Ryan asks. 'What are you doing down here?'

CHAPTER SIXTEEN

Ryan tugs at my arm roughly as he pulls me through the darkened tunnel. He moves forward quickly and with purpose, not slowing when we reach the tighter sections or when I stumble in the darkness. It seems as though he knows his way well and he's obviously not scared of the tight space we move through.

'Of all the stupid things...' he mutters to himself. I only just catch his words and they make me feel like I've been doused in a bucket of ice cold water.

The silence between us stretches and we continue to stumble wordlessly in the darkness. He obviously thinks I'm an idiot, but right now I couldn't care what he thinks. He's been lying to me about who he is, and that's clearly far worse.

Once we're out of the tunnel he veers away from the route I'd initially followed. Instead we enter a corridor that is much darker than the others I'd walked through earlier. The ground is more uneven and it seems to get colder the further in we walk.

I find it difficult to keep calm as the darkness continues to engulf us. My body goes rigid and I can feel panic beginning to slowly take form at the edges of my awareness. I imagine the panic is like a dark black sludge, slowly covering me, waiting for a crack in my façade through which it can seep in. I'm determined though, and refuse to let it get to me.

Eventually Ryan slows his rapid pace. As he does, he pulls out a torch from his pocket. I clearly hear the sound of a switch being flicked and a bright white circle of light appears on the ceiling. He shines the beam up and down the hallway, then, seeing we're alone, he stops and finally lets go of my hand.

'So you're an official?' I ask, gently rubbing the spot where he'd grasped me so tightly. It certainly would explain a lot.

He shines the torch directly at my face and I put up my hand to stop the light from blinding me. The light quickly drops from my face to the ground as Ryan folds his arms across his chest. 'Not quite...' he replies, keeping his voice low. 'Look, there's no time to explain. We have to get you out of here.'

'So you're not going to arrest me?'

He raises his eyebrows at me; as though he's offended I had to ask. 'Not tonight,' is all he says. 'What are you doing in the Old Wing anyway?'

'My friend was taken tonight,' I say. 'I don't really even know how it happened, but I somehow ended up here. Then, when I heard the voices of the officials I followed them and they led me to the entrance.'

He continues to look at me disapprovingly, like I'm the world's biggest idiot. I probably am. There's not that many people left to compete with.

'I thought maybe Sebastian had been taken here,' I say, my voice breaking as a tear escapes down my cheek.

Ryan sighs and steps closer to give me a hug. Once his arms are around me I begin to cry. Like *really,* embarrassingly cry. I can't help it. Being shown kindness when I'm so sad only seems to make my sorrow worse. It was easier when he was being mean.

'It's alright.' He rubs my back and makes gentle, soothing noises.

My tears begin to lessen and I step back from him embarrassed. I feel uncomfortable sharing such a broken part of myself with him. I trust him, but I don't want him to think I'm so fragile.

'Are you okay?' he asks softly.

'I'm not sure if I'll ever be okay. But the crying has stopped if that's what you're asking.'

He clears his throat and gives me an awkward pat on the shoulder. 'You need to go back now,' he says. I nod, quite happy to comply. 'This area isn't safe. Please promise me you won't come back here.'

'I won't.' He doesn't need to convince me to leave this place. I'd just about do anything to get out of here.

He watches me for a moment as though analysing my reaction. Finally he gives a brief nod that suggests he's satisfied I won't return and he turns to continue down the hallway.

'Do you know where they take the tainted?' I ask, catching up with him.

'That's not something I can discuss with you,' he responds quite formally. His answer isn't 'no,' so he must know something.

I touch his arm lightly. 'Please Ryan. I need to know.'

He almost growls when he turns towards me. 'I can't say anything,' he says tightly. 'Come on, I'll walk you to the exit of the Old Wing. We'll be in here for hours if we keep stopping this way.'

I drop my hand down to my side and suppress the tears that threaten to breach the surface of my eyes again. 'Could you at least tell me if he'll be okay?'

He pauses. I can almost see his mind whirring as he thinks it through.

'Your friend is still alive.'

It takes over an hour to get back to the East Wing and by the time I reach the Atrium it's the middle of the night. My feet are on autopilot as they drag me towards the North Wing, but I pause when I approach one of the surface screens. I stare at the turbulent wasteland and try to imagine where Sebastian is right now, and whether he's somewhere where he can see the stars tonight—if that's even possible. I wonder if he's with his mum and his sister. I hope more than anything he is. That they're taking care of him, wherever they are, and he will get well soon.

As I stare at the wastes a part of me considers what my life will be like now he's gone. The thought is haunting though and I quickly dismiss it.

My CommCuff buzzes as a message comes through with a request that I attend therapy in the morning. I groan as I read the message. It's hardly a request, more of a demand as I have no choice in the matter. I rub my eyes tiredly and decide it's time to stop my exhausted, delirious musings and go home.

When I get back to my quarters I attempt to quietly open the door, not wanting to disturb Quinn who must surely be sleeping by now. To my surprise she stands in the middle of the room pacing, her face lined with worry. Seeing me, standing in the doorway, she rushes over.

'I've been so worried Elle!' She grabs my shoulders and shakes me slightly. 'When you ran away I didn't know where you might go. Adam was just lying there crumpled on the floor. I couldn't just leave him ... but then you didn't come back and I tried to look for you in all your usual places, but you weren't anywhere.' She drops her arms from my shoulders and stands back.

'Where have you been?' she asks with 'mother-like' concern. I try to gauge how she is feeling before I respond. Her face is drained of its usual colour, her eyes are bloodshot and her hair is a complete mess—always a sure sign she's not doing too well. She looks how I feel and I hate to think how I must look.

It's clear she's already been so worried about me. I can't tell her about the Old Wing or about Ryan when she's in this state. She doesn't need to know.

I shrug in response to her question and say, 'I was just walking around. I'm not really too sure where I was.' At least there's an element of truth in that.

She gathers me up in a hug. 'You poor thing,' she murmurs in my ear. When she pulls away she examines me closely. 'How do you feel?'

'I've been better,' I say wearily.

Her eyebrows crease with concern. 'Look at you. You're dead on your feet.' With that, I'm swiftly ordered to go to bed.

I hadn't realised how tired I was. How could one evening drain me so completely? It doesn't take much coaxing to get me into bed. Once sleep is mentioned exhaustion overwhelms me, and I can barely stand. As I curl into a ball under the covers, I am calmed by one clear thought. Sebastian is still alive.

CHAPTER SEVENTEEN

The therapist's office is quite different to the rest of the ARC. Most places down here have a clinical feel to them, with rigid metal chairs and tables, or stark white walls and floors. This room, however, is all beige tones. It has a warm, soft feel to it and seems suspiciously inviting.

As I enter, the therapist introduces herself as Dr. Foster, though she asks me to call her Simone. Her voice is pleasant, and similar to the other therapists I've seen, in that it almost has a soothing quality to it.

It doesn't matter how understanding her voice is though, I already see this woman as the enemy and don't trust her.

She offers me a seat on one of the beige leather chairs in the room and then proceeds to sit down in a similar one across from me. The seat is incredibly comfortable, but I cannot bring myself to relax into it. My back stays rigid and my eyes are alert. The session hasn't even started yet and I'm mentally geared up as though I'm about to be attacked.

'Is it alright if I call you Elle?' Dr. Foster asks, as she gets comfortable in her seat. She's younger than the other therapists I've had before, though it's been a while since I've been close enough to anyone taken to warrant any sort of therapy.

Simone watches me, waiting patiently for my response. I can't be certain how understanding she is though. It's difficult to distinguish her patient, waiting face from what could be an irritated or angry face. Her eyes have held the same look of consideration and interest since the moment I entered the room.

I try to avoid eye contact with her. I've always had this irrational fear that with one look a therapist will see into the depths of my soul. Instead, I stare at the bookcase that runs across the wall behind her, feigning interest in the titles that run along the many book spines.

I don't want to be here, and I definitely don't want to answer any questions she has. Unfortunately, unless I want to spend my life in therapy, I know I have to engage with this woman.

'Elle's fine,' I respond to Simone indifferently.

It's funny how two simple words can send her into a frenzy of typing on her tablet. Was it my tone of voice? My lack of eye contact? Maybe the words used alone are worthy of analysis?

After a few seconds she looks up from her tablet. 'So, what brings you to therapy today?' she asks, as if she doesn't already know the answer.

I highly doubt that a message on my cuff is the answer she wants to hear, so I tell her the truth. 'My friend Sebastian was ... taken,' I say, my voice stumbling over the word 'taken.'

She nods her head up and down several times before she continues. 'You were fostered with his family for several years. Would you say that you were close to Sebastian?'

My fingers, which are clenched in tight little fists on my lap, seem to clench impossibly tighter upon hearing his name. 'We were close,' I respond quietly. Even closer than she knows I imagine, but I daren't tell her just how much he means to me. Especially not when I have so much difficulty admitting the truth of how I feel to myself.

My eyes drift over and settle on the lampshade that sits on the small round table next to her chair. It emits a soft golden glow, quite different to the other lights in the ARC. Like the rest of the room the light seems to radiate a feeling of safety and comfort. It's as though they think one golden light will make me open up to some stranger about my deepest, darkest secrets.

'What would you like to get out of your sessions with me?' Simone asks.

I sit in silence as I consider her words. I don't want her help, but saying that will only prolong this process. I learnt that the hard way with the therapist who saw me after April was taken.

Assuming this woman can help me, what do I want? She can't change that Sebastian was taken and there's nothing she or anyone else can do to bring him back. What can talking to her give me that action cannot?

'I want to be able to move on,' I say quietly. The words are hard to say and make me feel like I've plunged a dagger into my chest. Staying here and moving on was never the plan if one of us was taken.

Simone nods and starts quickly tapping away at her tablet again. I think I've given her the answer she wanted, but it feels a far cry away from what I want inside.

After therapy I head to school, which is bad. *Very* bad. People watch me constantly. They watch me in class, between classes and they even stare at me as I wash my hands in the bathroom. It's like I'm some horrible accident. They know it's bad and they shouldn't look, but they just can't seem to tear their eyes away.

'Screw 'em,' Gemma says to me at lunch. 'If they want to stare they obviously haven't got anything better to do.' With Gemma by my side, glaring at anyone who even thinks about looking at me, the staring is almost bearable.

Unfortunately it's not just the staring that's disturbing. It's the sickly sweet kindness from everyone, especially the teachers. Even Kate is being nice and it seriously makes me want to vomit.

Eventually the bell rings signalling the end of the day. I feel a weight lift off my shoulders as I exit school. I don't need to keep pretending to be okay.

Gemma catches up with me as I slowly traipse down the hallway towards the Atrium.

'How are you after today?' she asks.

I raise my eyebrows as though she's just asked the silliest question ever.

'Yeah people suck,' she says. 'So, no basketball tonight?'

'No. I'm behind on my community service hours. Besides, I can't really bring myself to face it,' I reply. 'I'm just so worried about him Gem!'

'I'm certain nothing bad happens to the tainted. They just have to live somewhere else is all.' She says it in an attempt to comfort me, but her repetition of the Council line isn't exactly cheering.

'It doesn't change he's no longer here,' I respond quietly. There's nothing she can say that will make *that* fact better. I glance over my shoulder to check the corridor is clear before I continue. 'Have you ever wondered if it's possible to go after the tainted?'

Gemma grabs my arm roughly pulling me to a stop. She glances over her own shoulder before turning back to me. 'Elle that's crazy! Don't say that... Don't even think that!' Her voice is quiet, but her words are firm. 'No one follows after them. It's too dangerous, you could get sick too!'

'Sorry—yeah, you're right—of course you're right.' I shake my head at the idiocy of what I've just said, but I feel confused. While it sounds idiotic, for some reason, it doesn't seem like such a stupid idea.

Gemma is reassured by my response and lets go of the firm grip she has on my arm. She still seems upset though. Just the mere mention of attempting to find someone tainted has her giving me the silent treatment—I guess most people would react the same way. As we continue walking I can't stop thinking about it. I should be terrified at the idea of trying to leave, but instead the idea comforts me and for the first time since Sebastian left I feel hopeful.

I SAY goodbye to Gemma at the Atrium and continue on to the Aged Care Ward, where I'm assigned to do my hours today. The ward is shunted to the far corner of the Hospital Wing, so it's a long trek to reach it from school.

The entrance to the ward is fairly nondescript. A plain pair of swinging doors and a small plastic sign on the wall with the ward name embossed across it. I take a moment to compose myself before entering. While reading to the elderly is not my dream assignment, one of the teachers at school recommended it, as it would look good on my apprenticeship application. So today marks the first of many community service hours for me over here.

The doors swing easily open and I walk into a sparse reception. A simple desk and several plastic bucket seats lined along the wall are all that occupy the space. The whole place reeks of disinfectant.

A small, middle-aged woman sits behind the reception desk. Her head is bowed down over a tablet and she appears to be completely absorbed in whatever she is reading.

'Hello,' I say, as I approach the desk. I hate having to interrupt her when she's obviously so riveted to her tablet screen, especially when even to my own ears my voice is completely lacking any enthusiasm.

'Can I help you?' she asks bluntly. It's clear from her tight set lips and her piercing stare that this woman is not to be messed with. It takes me a second to recover from the shock of her brusque attitude.

'I'm from the school,' I finally say. 'I'm here to log some community service hours.'

'Name?' the woman requests sternly.

'Elle Winters.'

'Sign in here.' She points towards the CommuSensor on her computer, before focusing down on her tablet again. I bump my cuff against the sensor and wait for further instructions.

'You're in room 36 with Mrs. Mayberry today. The room's just down the end of that hallway and on the right,' she says, still looking at her tablet and shaking her hand over in the direction of a corridor directly to the left of her desk.

After several seconds of silence I realise this is all the guidance she'll be giving me for my session today. I say thank you quietly to the woman, not wishing to disturb her again, and set off in the direction she had waved to.

When I reach the door with the shiny metal number 36 on it I stop. The door is open and inside I can see an old woman lying back on her bed, sleeping quietly. I go to walk into the room, but my feet are cemented to the ground and they refuse to budge. I feel torn. I'm here to sit with this woman, but I can't bring myself to walk in there and disturb her when she looks so peaceful.

Before I can make up my mind, the door across the hallway bursts open. Two male nurses appear, attempting to drag an old man out of his room and into the hallway.

'C'mon Dr. Wilson, you can't put your testing off any longer,' one of them shouts over the man's desperate struggles. I clamber backwards to the opposite wall.

'No!' he screams. 'No! You can't take me!' he yells even louder. 'I *know* about the tainted. I practically diagnosed it! Don't you think I'd *know* if I was tainted?'

'Yes Dr. Wilson, but we still have to follow protocol,' the nurse says.

The old man continues to struggle and then his eyes lock on mine. 'Don't let them take me,' he pleads with me. The nurse roughly tugs at his arms.

'No!' The old man begins yelling again. He lunges forward and somehow manages to break free of the nurses' grasp causing all three of them to fall to the ground. The man scrambles to his feet and then stumbles towards me with surprising speed. I'm terrified, but rooted to the spot as he grabs me by the arms.

'Don't let them take me,' he whispers again, as he leans in close to my face. I can clearly see the panic in his eyes. 'Don't let them take me. I'm not taint...'

Before the old man can finish one of the nurses rips him away from me and pins him against the wall. The other nurse brings out a syringe and injects the man in the arm. Immediately his whole body begins to slouch and his yelling dies down to a quiet mutter, as he allows himself to be dragged away.

One of the nurses looks over his shoulder at me as he leaves. His eyes are threatening and my feet, which had moments ago felt glued to the floor, begin walking like they have a mind of their own. Before I know it I'm running back through the reception.

The woman at the desk shouts something after me, but I don't listen. Instead I make a beeline for the exit. People stare as I run through the hospital. I can feel their eyes burning into my skin with disapproval.

More than once I hear yells of 'slow down' or 'no running,' but I need to get away from here as quickly as I can.

Once I'm out of the Hospital Wing I fall against a wall, leaning one hand against it for support. Short, shallow breaths grip me and I am unable to fill my lungs. My chest is tight and feels like it's burning inside. I firmly press one of my hands against it as I try to calm down, but I still can't seem to breathe.

I close my eyes tightly shut and try to force deep breaths of air back into my lungs. With my voice quaking, I count to ten. As I count my breathing slows and gradually the air manages to make it down into my lungs.

When my breath is steady I open my eyes again. The hallway is empty and I feel relieved no one witnessed my breakdown. I'm quick to huddle my arms around my body and begin the walk back to my room.

I've always heard they use brute force when people refuse to attend their testing. But having seen it with my own eyes, especially on someone so old, has shaken me to the core.

I'm grateful to find my room empty when I return. Quinn has been so kind to me since Sebastian was taken, but she looks at me like I'm a fragile piece of porcelain china teetering precariously over the edge of a table.

I throw myself on my bed and burrow my way under the sheets. For a minute I stare at the ceiling and try to imagine where Sebastian is right now, but my thoughts are dark and bring me too much pain. I roll up into a ball and try to block them out, desperate to simply fall into a peaceful, dreamless sleep. I toss and turn restlessly though. My whole body is covered in sweat and I can't seem to completely nod off, but I'm unable to stay completely awake either.

As I drift turbulently in and out of consciousness I am aware of Sebastian's voice echoing through my mind.

'You promised you would come for me,' his voice whispers, betrayed.

CHAPTER EIGHTEEN

The week passes slowly. At school people still gawk at me, but after only a few days the staring has stopped altogether. It's as though they've all forgotten Sebastian is gone and there's no longer a reason to treat me like I'm fragile.

I guess that's how people cope down here. You learn to forget the ones that are taken because if you dwell on it you lose any ability to function normally.

There's nothing I want more than to forget him, but the longer he is gone the more my heart seems to ache at his absence. Several times I've found myself instinctively searching for his face in the dinner hall or looking up to share a joke with him, only to find the seat next to me empty. Yesterday morning I'd been halfway to his quarters before it had hit me he was no longer there.

I'm a mess. I suppose that's why I'm here in therapy. It's to be expected.

Still, I need to stop thinking about him.

A cold shiver runs down my back and I wrap my arms across my chest. I *need* to forget, but all I can think about is the promise I made. How I said I would come for him.

'How are you feeling today?' Simone asks me.

I shrug my shoulders and continue to look determinedly at one of the books that are open on the table next to her. This week has been hell and I'm not coping, but I don't want her to know how hard I'm taking it. She continues waiting for me to say something and the silence makes me uncomfortable, so I say, 'I feel guilty.'

'Why do you feel guilty?'

I sigh and look down into my hands. 'Because I can't forget him. I know I'm supposed to, but I can't.'

'Why do you feel you need to forget him?' She's stopped typing on her tablet and is watching me closely.

'Isn't that what everyone wants? Isn't that how I'm supposed to move on?' I bite down on my lip as I feel tears beginning to well in my eyes. I take a deep breath and try to focus on controlling them. I refuse to break down in front of this woman.

She pauses before she answers. 'I don't think anyone would ever expect you to forget about your friend.'

I curl my legs up on the chair and start playing with my pendant as I think. Her answer surprises me. I thought forgetting the tainted was exactly what the Council wanted. 'Then how do I move on?'

'How do you think I would answer that question?' she asks kindly.

I peer up at her. She looks like she's genuinely interested in my answer, so I take a moment to consider it. 'I think you'd tell me I have to let go and accept he's gone.'

She nods, but I can't tell if she's indicating it's the right answer or if she's just showing she's listening.

'Why would I suggest that do you think?'

'I don't know,' I respond. 'Aren't you the therapist here?'

She laughs lightly. 'Yes, but it may help to come to some of these conclusions yourself.'

'Right,' I mumble, still with no clue how to answer her question.

Simone moves on from that though and asks me something different. 'How does Sebastian leaving make you feel?' she asks.

Empty is the first thing that comes to mind, but I quickly realise as much as that's true, there's something that feels much worse for me than that.

'Powerless,' I answer. 'There was nothing I could do to stop him getting sick.' There's also nothing I can do to get him back, but I keep my mouth shut about that one.

Silence hovers over the room and I almost think I can see a glint of sympathy in Simone's eyes, but she quickly looks away, glancing down at her CommuCuff and then back up again. 'We're at the end of our allotted time for today. You've taken some positive steps this session in opening up to me. How do you think our talk today went?'

'Good?' I say, well, ask. I have no idea how to gauge how today went.

'I'd like to set you some homework for the next week that I think may help. Why don't you think of some things in your life that you can change, rather than the ones you can't?'

Homework? Really? I want to groan. 'Okay,' I respond, not bothering to keep the displeasure from my voice.

She smiles and stands to show me out. 'I'll see you in a couple of days. You'll get a reminder message on your cuff the night before.'

The door closes behind me and I feel relieved to be finished with Simone for the day. I never know how much to say in those sessions and I don't want to say the wrong thing and get in trouble. Sometimes I worry she'll see how messed up I really am and I'll be stuck in therapy for life.

The therapist's office is right around the corner from the Hospital Wing, so I quickly find myself standing in front of it. Ever since Sebastian was taken my heart seems to stutter in my chest every time I see it. In just one week I'll be entering the hospital for my own testing. The thought makes me happy in a way.

I have my community service hours in the Aged Care Ward again today. I hesitate at the entrance though, and worry about what to expect. Surely everything will be fine and I won't experience a repeat of last week?

My hours are longer today to make up for my disappearance last week. Once upon a time I'd feel annoyed about extra hours. I'd be pissed about missing basketball or I'd moan because it was going to be boring. Now though? I feel nothing. I dig my hands into my pockets as I make my way inside. Feeling nothing is worse than all the bad feelings put together.

When I arrive at the Aged Care Ward the same lady is behind the desk again. 'Can I help you?' she asks sourly.

'Yes. Elle Winters, I'm here for my community service hours.'

She looks me up and down, her nose almost turning up with disapproval. 'Oh you're actually going to do them this week?' she says.

I bump my cuff against the CommuSensor to sign in.

'You're with Mrs. Mayberry again,' she continues, her voice turning quite spiteful. 'I thought you'd appreciate it seeing as you were unable to sit with her last week.'

I nod tightly at her and then walk down the corridor to the left of the desk.

'Room 36,' she calls out behind me, her voice sickly sweet.

I don't look back.

When I reach room 36 I peer inside, hoping to see Mrs. Mayberry sitting up in bed or busying herself over at the small table and chairs. Instead I find her sleeping again. My shoulders slouch with disappointment. I'd been looking forward to the distraction.

There's a cough from one of the rooms across the hallway behind me and I turn towards the noise. The cough comes again and I wander over to the room directly opposite Mrs. Mayberry's.

Standing just outside the doorway of room 37, I can see inside sits the man who'd been struggling against the nurses last week. The first thing that hits me about him is he doesn't seem deranged and angry like he was the last time I was here. In fact, from where I'm standing, there doesn't seem to be anything wrong with him at all. It's hard to believe he's the same person who I'd seen making such a commotion seven days ago.

Sitting at the table, playing on his tablet, he simply seems like a bored old man who was shafted into the care facility.

I look up and down the hallway before stepping into the room. He turns to me as I enter and switches his tablet off, placing it down on the table.

'Dr. Wilson?' I say, uncertain I have his name correct.

'Ah company!' he says cheerfully. I ease my way closer to the table. I don't see any recognition in his eyes and I wonder if he even remembers what happened last week.

'Sit, sit.' He pulls his shoulders back and smiles as he waves me towards the seat opposite him. He is straight into entertainment mode. I can only assume he doesn't get many visitors.

'So my dear, whom do I have the pleasure of speaking with today?' he asks, sitting slightly straighter and crossing one leg over the other.

'Elle Winters,' I reply.

'Well Miss Winters, please do tell me how you ended up in the Asteroid Refugee Compound?'

'Oh,' I respond, taking a second to gather my thoughts. I am definitely thrown by his direct and obtrusive question.

'I was young when I came. I don't really remember.' I laugh faintly and say, almost to myself, 'I haven't heard the ARC called by that name in a long time.'

I was only two years old when the asteroid hit. And it was true what I had said—I don't remember how I came to be here. But I do have flashes of memories, snippets of the story I cannot start or finish.

The sound of people's desperate cries as they pushed and shoved their way towards the mountain that towered over us is a sound you could never forget. But the most vivid memory I have is how I felt. I was lost and my parents were missing. It was a gut wrenching, sickening feeling that haunts me whenever I think about it.

I also remember there had been a man. I can't remember what he looked like, but I do remember how comforting holding his hand had felt. He had made me feel so safe and secure when the world was falling to pieces around me. He saved me and I wouldn't be here if it hadn't been for him.

Dr. Wilson is nodding to himself as he mutters about orphans and the tragedy of it all.

'Yes, I guess we can't all be so fortunate as to have been selectively picked for our expertise, and potential for furthering the future of the human race,' he says, quite delighted with himself and his achievement.

'So, Dr. Wilson, what kind of doctor are you?'

'Oh you're sweet,' he says. 'But I don't practice medicine anymore. I was, back in the day, a pathologist. Specialised in rare diseases.' He frowns slightly at the end of the sentence, like something troubles him about what he has said.

'So you must've been involved with the *tainted* then?' I ask slowly, as I recall his ravings from the previous week.

'Yes, yes. I was a part of all that. Did some of my best work with the tainted. Ah, those were good times.' I try to cover a grimace. I can see why he no longer practices if he views dealing with a disease that has taken so many of our people away from us as a 'good time'.

I attempt to gently probe him more with questions. 'So, you dealt with them?' I confirm.

'Yes, yes,' he replies, as he looks down into the glass of water he cradles in his lap. 'Such a complex mutation, so intricate and beautiful. Oh and with incredibly unique symptoms!'

I feel a lump in my throat and the hairs on my arms stand on end at the sound of the word. *Symptoms*?

'What kinds of symptoms?'

'Well, there was this one tainted boy and he could...' He stops mid sentence and looks at me suspiciously, as though unsure whether he should continue.

'Hmm, let's not get into all that,' he decides. 'Unpleasant business. Besides, my medical days are far behind me. My mind isn't what it used to be.' He chuckles nervously, tapping his head with a long, fragile finger.

I try to laugh along with him, but I'm not convinced by his supposed confusion. After he stops laughing he still looks at me untrustingly; he's not convinced by me either.

'You must've had a large lab? For all of your patients?' I ask, trying a different tact. His eyes light up at the question and he looks relieved we have quickly moved on to a much safer topic.

'Oh yes,' he responds. 'It was in the Hospital Wing. They gave me free range in those days.' His eyes glass over as he reminisces on the 'good old days.'

'Gosh if it hadn't been for me, we never would've found that marker in the blood. And we definitely wouldn't have been able to test for it. Come to think of it, we never would've known about the signal symptoms you get leading up to it either!' he says proudly.

'Signal symptoms?' I ask. 'I thought it was through the yearly testing that people who are affected are discovered?' I sit on the edge of my seat. I'm trying desperately not to sound too eager or too keen, but everything he's saying is making it very difficult.

'Well, initially it was simply the test. But after I found out the infection begins with a fever we were able to diagnose the tainted sooner.'

I take a second, attempting to absorb what he's said. 'It sounds like you were the glue that held it all together,' I say.

'I was! The *Council* should be grateful for all that I've done for them!' he replies, anger seeping into his voice as he utters the word 'Council.'

He begins to bluster about the Council and I sit back in my chair slightly. I've struck a nerve, and not a good one.

'Did you know *I* was the one who set up *tainted* protocol. *I* was the reason we could ensure our survival. The *Council*, pah! Those idiots didn't know what had hit them.

'They still have no idea what's hit them! And *they* think they can just shut me in here? Take all of my hard work from me?' His hands begin shaking as his voice builds.

'And *they* have the gall to start sending people away! Those patients were no danger. The *Council* got scared. They figured they'd send them off and pretend they don't exist. Great solution when it's mostly the young that get infected! Ha! There'll be no one left if they keep at it!'

Dr. Wilson isn't the only one shaking now. 'Surely you must know where they go?' I ask, my voice unsteady, as my desperation to know the truth begins to seep through the cracks in my outwardly calm façade.

The anger seeps away from his eyes and sadness seems to replace it. He rubs the arch of his nose, wearily.

'If only I knew,' he says. 'My own grandson was taken a few years back. I may have been in charge of diagnosis, but I have no idea where they went from there. I can only hope it's somewhere better than here.'

'We all do,' I say quietly.

WHEN I ARRIVE BACK at home, I find Quinn sitting on her bed reading. I quickly close the door behind me then turn to her. She looks up at me with the same sad smile she's given me all week, but for the first time I don't feel the despair that smile deserves.

'I have to find him,' I say, finally uttering the words that have been tumbling through my mind.

'What are you talking ab—'

'Sebastian, I promised him I'd come for him. I have to find a way to get him back!'

She looks at me like I'm talking complete nonsense. Maybe I am? I've been thinking about it on some level since the moment I heard the news Sebastian was gone. But going after him hadn't seemed possible until I sat down with Dr. Wilson. Talking with him had finally cemented it in my mind and I know I will never be able to move on if I don't at least try.

'Elle...' she says, her voice full of sorrow.

'Whatever you think you're about to say, stop. I made a promise to him and I'm not about to break it.'

She stands and walks over to me. 'Elle you've been through so much this last week.' She takes my hands in hers and squeezes them. 'I know it's been tough, but he wouldn't expect you to follow after him, promise or not.'

I step back, shaking my hands free of hers. 'It's not just about the promise Quinn. I have to do this. I haven't been myself since he left. I haven't been anyone. I've been an empty shell with no one home. I've been just like Adam and I refuse to turn into a shadow like him.

'I've had enough. There have been too many people ripped away from us now. The list has grown so long that I've lost count. But knowing I'm going to go after him? I feel better. More determined. It's the right thing to do.'

She frowns and I can tell she's trying to think of another argument for why trying to rescue him is a bad idea.

'The therapist told me to focus on the things I can change rather than those I can't. I can't change that he was taken. I can change the fact that we're apart by going after him.'

'I doubt that's what she meant...'

'I don't need to hear it,' I tell her before she starts on me again. 'You either support my decision or you don't, but there's no changing my mind.'

'What are you planning to do?' she asks, her voice curious as she changes tactics on me. There's no way she's changed her mind so quickly, and her eyes are wary, making me feel like she's kindly guiding me towards a trap.

I ignore the suspicion I feel and focus on her question. When I had asked it myself my mind had automatically gone to Ryan. I suspect he knows exactly what happens to the tainted. But more than that, I think he's tied up with it somehow. There's no way he will tell me though, otherwise he would've answered my questions the other night.

I already know the entrance is closed up and the top floors of the ARC have been abandoned.

Every option that has run through my mind has been as unconvincing as the next. They're all safe options. Unlikely options. Options that will keep me here indefinitely.

I'm left with only one possibility and Quinn's not going to like it at all.

'There's only one way I'm going to find Sebastian. I have to be *taken*.'

CHAPTER NINETEEN

'You're going to get yourself killed,' Quinn fumes at me. She's spent the last twenty minutes pacing up and down the small space in our room, throwing her arms in the air and muttering to herself. So while it's not what I want to be hearing, I'm kind of glad she's at least talking now.

'Seriously Elle, are you crazy? We have absolutely no idea what happens to the tainted when they're taken. I won't have you risking your life!'

I sit and allow her to vent, knowing eventually she has to run out of steam.

'I mean, Sebastian could already be dead. Do you really want to follow him to the grave?' I continue to calmly watch her. Anything I might say will only add fuel to her already raging fire.

For the first time since Sebastian was taken I finally have clarity and resolve. I know what I need to do and Quinn will eventually see that.

'How do you suppose you'll even get taken? You can't just walk up to the hospital and tell them you'd like to leave now.'

'I'm not certain, but what if I can somehow fake the blood test?' I say.

'Oh well done. Brilliant plan Elle. That should definitely work.' Quinn's tone of voice is completely sarcastic.

'I didn't say it was perfect. I just think that's going to be the best way,' I respond.

'What if they do something to you? For all we know the tainted could be tested on. They could be placed somewhere to slowly allow their mutations to take over and kill them. They could actually just kill them! I know you don't want to hear this, but there's a possibility Sebastian is already dead, and if you follow him you may end up the same.'

'That's a risk I'm willing to take,' I say, as confidently as I can.

She looks completely unconvinced. 'What if they send the *tainted* up to the surface? Ditch them outside, shut the doors behind them and leave them to fend for themselves. You would have no chance of survival. It would be a cold, slow death, completely alone. You would be stupid not to be afraid.'

'We don't know what they do,' I say. 'But I'm more afraid of the regret I will feel for the rest of my life if I don't at least try.'

'You don't have enough information. We don't even know what blood type you are—'

'O positive,' I mutter. She blatantly ignores this and continues.

'The thought of you attempting to leave makes me sick to my stomach. I don't want you to do this.'

'But...'

'I can't support this! It's crazy. I don't want you getting hurt.'

She bends down to pick up her bag, slings it over her shoulder and walks to the door.

'I never thought I'd see the day when I'd have to say this, but I won't help you. You're on your own.'

Quinn doesn't come back for hours. As it gets later I begin to worry I've really done it this time. I shouldn't have told her. I'd been crazy to think she'd support this, let alone that she'd help me do it.

A knock raps on the door and I feel a rush of relief as I get up to answer it. She's come back.

I'm startled when I open the door to find Adam Scott standing in the doorway. His face is heavy with exhaustion, like he hasn't slept in years.

'Hi Elle. How're you doing?' His voice is just as weary as his face.

'Yeah, okay,' I say. 'Sorry I ran off the other night. It was just, you know ... a lot.' He nods in agreement, he obviously understands.

We stand there in awkward silence for a moment. 'Oh, did you want to come in?' I ask, opening the door further.

'No, I'm fine. I just came by to give you something.' He glances down at the tablet he clutches firmly to his chest.

'I'm not sure if you know this, but once someone is taken they're allowed to record a goodbye. They gave this to me the other day.' He reluctantly passes the tablet over to me. 'Towards the end of the recording, Sebastian left a goodbye to you,' he says. 'It's about seven minutes in. I'll leave it here with you, but if you wouldn't mind returning it when you're done? It's all I have left...'

'Of course,' I murmur. I don't really know what else to say. I had no idea. I guess Adam didn't want to unnecessarily upset me when April was taken and that's why I never saw hers?

'Well, that was all.' He looks down the hallway as though to leave, but then turns back to me. 'I'm sorry things never ended up the way we'd hoped. It was never the same once you left too—n-not that I blame you!' He scratches his head as if frustrated and I get the impression his words aren't coming out how he means them. 'I just want you to know that if you ever need to talk or just want to visit ... my door's always open.'

I step forward and give him a hug.

'I'm here for you too Adam,' I say. The words feel like a lie though, and a lump of guilt develops in the pit of my stomach. If I succeed in what I'm planning I won't be here for long.

Once Adam has left I take a seat on my bed and stare down at the black screen, almost scared to turn it on. We'd left so much unsaid...

The home screen is empty except for the movie file labelled Sebastian Scott. I double tap the file, hardly able to believe I get to see his face again.

The video file opens and shows Sebastian sitting in a plain grey room. He looks tired and his face is drawn, but he doesn't look particularly unhappy. He looks up and into the camera, attempting to put on a brave face.

'Hi Dad,' he says. The sound of his voice wrenches my gut. 'Damn! I really didn't see this one coming,' he mutters.

I jump forward to the seven-minute mark on the recording. I don't want to pry. Especially when it's so obvious how much Adam cherishes this video.

I press play for the second time. Sebastian is in the middle of a sentence. '...so you won't have to worry about me,' he says. 'Just know I love you Dad and everything is going to be okay!'

I've never seen the softer side of Sebastian and Adam's relationship. They never really talked much and I'd always assumed it was more of an unspoken bond. It's nice to see how much he cared.

'So if you wouldn't mind passing this along Dad? I'd like to say something to Elle now.' He sits slightly straighter and the look in his eyes makes my heart pound faster.

'Hey Elle,' he begins. 'Bet you're really pissed at me right about now. Hell, I'm really pissed at me right about now, so that makes two of us.' For once he's wrong, I'm not pissed off at him. I'm pissed off at pretty much anyone but him at this point.

'I don't really know where to begin. There are so many things I want to say to you. I guess I'll just go for the important stuff.' He laughs before he continues. 'And I can pretty much say whatever I want because I'm never going to see you again.' A frown crosses his forehead as he says that. He takes a deep breath and looks up at the camera timidly. He looks like he might be blushing or maybe he's just nervous, I can't tell which.

'I'm ... well I'm annoyed I never told you how I feel about you. You're the best friend I could ever hope for and I'm fairly certain I'm going to regret not being brave enough to come after you at the dance the other night for the rest of my life. However long that may be.' He mutters the last sentence and then his eyes flick apprehensively off camera before slowly returning back to it.

'But that isn't what's important. What's important is I want more than anything for you to be happy. I don't want you to worry about me or to try and come find me. I want you to be safe, just like we always talked about.'

I am physically shaking at this point and I can feel my eyes glistening with unshed tears. More than ever, I can't believe he's gone.

'Well, that's my time up. Please stay safe Elle.'

The recording stops and the home screen returns. I stare at it blankly, uncertain how to react. I hadn't expected to see his face or hear his voice again. Now I have, it feels impossible to let him go.

I open up the recording and watch it again, then again. I am just in the middle of re-watching for about the fifth time when Quinn comes back into the room. I quickly pause it as she enters.

She walks directly to her bed with her head firmly turned away, as though she intends to ignore me, but she notices the way I clutch the tablet and asks, 'What have you got there?'

'A message from Sebastian.'

'What do you mean?' She cocks her head and looks curiously at the tablet.

'They let him record a message when he was taken. His dad just gave it to me.'

'Really?' she says, surprised.

'You didn't know?'

She shakes her head. 'No. I've never received one... How was it?'

'Good... Well, okay... Actually it was really confusing,' I admit. 'We'd said we'd come for each other if one of us were taken. Then he goes and tells me he doesn't want me to. Does he really not want me to come after him?'

She walks over to the bed and sits down next to me. 'Maybe when it came down to it, he didn't want to risk you getting hurt. Maybe he knows now how dangerous it is? He probably has a point you know. You shouldn't be risking yourself for him.'

I look at her uncertainly. I'd felt so confident about trying to go after him. How am I supposed to drop that? Could he really not want me to follow?

'Would you like me to watch it? Get a second opinion?' Quinn asks.

I clutch the tablet closer to my chest, feeling a sudden protectiveness over its contents. I feel possessive and irrational about it, like a two-year-old being asked to share her favourite toy.

'Do you want me to watch it?' she repeats calmly.

'Yes,' I say, shaking off my unreasonable attachment and passing over the tablet.

Quinn takes it and watches the entire recording in silence. As she watches her face is a placid mask, no emotions showing her thoughts on what Sebastian says. When it stops she is quiet for several minutes and then she slowly begins talking.

'Well it sounds like he doesn't want you risking yourself to come after him,' she says sadly—she's probably loving this. 'Maybe you should reconsider whether following after him is a good idea?'

I look at the blank screen, perplexed. That can't be right. It just doesn't make sense. We both agreed we'd come for each other. I know he wouldn't change his mind. There has to be another explanation.

'These recordings ... why do they do them?' I ask, as though hoping it will explain Sebastian's change of heart.

'So they can say goodbye?' Quinn shrugs.

I huff out a breath and look away at the far wall. 'Yeah, they say goodbye, but it's not just goodbye is it? It's almost a reassurance they're going to be okay.' I put my head in my hands confused. 'Why would they do that?' I ask myself.

'To stop people from coming after them,' Quinn responds quietly. My head snaps up to look at her.

'Elle this is a bad idea,' she says, shaking her head. 'This isn't funny anymore—'

'It was never a joke.'

'You don't know what you could be getting yourself into...'

'Well I think it's about time I found out.'

CHAPTER TWENTY

I look in the mirror and stare at the bags that have slowly built under my eyes. The lack of sleep and my loss of appetite are beginning to show. My face looks haggard and I touch at my hollow cheeks with concern.

This week has gone too quickly. Time is going too quickly. It's already Thursday and the seconds seem to be slipping by faster and faster as my testing on Monday nears.

I glance down at the pile of books scattered chaotically across the end of my bed. Titles such as, 'The Quantifiable Effects of the Lysart Asteroid on the Human Genome' and 'The ARC: Time of Change' rest there. I checked them out of the library days ago hoping to find some answers, but they've given me no insight into the tainted. I still don't know nearly enough and, more importantly, have no idea how to fake a blood test.

It doesn't help that Quinn keeps shooting nervous glances my way when she thinks I'm not looking. It's obvious she's getting anxious, but I can't let it distract me. Even Gemma's begun to notice something's off with me and I've had to begin avoiding her at school.

I look down at my cuff and groan. I'm running late for school again. It should probably worry me, or even just put an extra spring in my step. A few weeks ago it doubtlessly would have. But all I can feel is anxiety, and worry—and an all-encompassing desperation to figure out how to fake my blood test.

It's this desperation that pushes me to walk straight past the corridor that will take me to school. It makes me forget any concerns Quinn may have aired about my safety. Instead it drives me towards the closest thing I've had to a lead—towards the Aged Care Ward to see Dr. Wilson.

'This is a nice surprise,' he says, when I walk into his room. 'I wasn't expecting any visitors this morning.' With slow, purposeful movements he folds the corner of the page in his open book. He lowers his glasses from his eyes and wraps the chain they dangle from around them several times before placing them on the table.

Today he wears his greys, like everyone else, but I notice a pair of old, tatty slippers peaking out from under the cuff of his pants.

'How are you Dr. Wilson?' I ask, taking a seat at the table across from him.

'Oh you know, plodding along well.'

'That's good,' I respond, pleasantly. I sit in silence staring at him, unable to fathom how I'm supposed to ask him the unaskable.

'Shouldn't you be at school?' he eventually asks, finally breaking the silence.

'Probably,' I mutter. Unfortunately school hasn't been getting too much face time with me over the last couple of weeks. 'I came today because I wanted to ask you some questions,' I explain.

He looks at me warily. 'Go on...'

I begin to fidget with my necklace. 'I wanted to know more about the *tainted*,' I say.

'What about them?' His voice is brusque and I start to feel like maybe this is going to be a waste of time.

'I want to know where they're taken.' I keep my voice as steady as possible so it doesn't reveal my desperation. I hold my breath as I wait for his response, but I can already tell from the guarded look in his eyes he's not about to tell me what I want to hear.

'I don't know anything about that,' he says.

'Please...'

'You know I'm beginning to feel quite tired. I think you should leave.' He nods his head at the door, but I don't move. He's my last chance. He has to help me.

'Fine,' he says. He leans over towards the large red button that calls for an attendant.

'You said your grandson was taken!' I blurt out. He stops. With his arm still reached out towards the button he freezes.

'And?' he slowly turns back and asks.

'I could help you get him back.'

'Why would you do that?'

'Because you're not the only person who's lost someone.'

He eases back into his chair and watches me as he deliberates. 'If you're not tainted you can't leave,' he finally says.

'I can if you help me.'

He ponders over this for a moment before he continues. 'I do want him back, but I can't help you.'

'Why not?'

He turns to stare at the wall, refusing to respond.

'You said yourself the tainted are no threat. The Council has taken so much from all of us and you know as well as anyone how hard it is to let go of the ones you've lost. I have nothing left to lose. Can you help me?'

'I'm afraid you misunderstand me. I don't know where they are taken. The little authority I had over the tainted is gone. Even if I wanted to, there's no way I can help you.'

'But you *know* things. There must be something you can do...'

'What I know is that what you want to do is dangerous. You could die.'

He sounds so certain that I can't believe that's all he knows. I obviously don't want to die—I'm not completely irrational. But I want to find Sebastian. I'm not afraid to face a little danger and to be honest I'd be stupid if I didn't expect some element of it.

'I accept there are risks,' I say, my voice sounding more confident than I feel.

He shakes his head at me. 'I fear you will regret this.'

I pause for a moment. Just a second to wonder if I'm jumping in too deep—to consider whether I'm going to be in way over my head. I quickly dismiss the thought. Sebastian is worth the risk.

'What do I have to do?' I ask.

'Like I said, I don't know where they go. I'm not sure how I can help.'

'That's okay,' I respond. 'I don't need to know where I'm going. I just need to fake the blood test.'

'Now that, I suppose, I can help you with. It won't be easy though. You'll need to get a hold of one of the tainted blood samples. They don't exactly leave them lying around.'

'Where are they kept?'

'The hospital has storage rooms on the third floor. You'll find everything you're looking for there.'

'Third floor. Okay I can do that.'

'You need to make sure you get a sample that's the right blood type—you do know your blood type?'

'Oh, ah, yes it's O-positive.'

'The vial you're after will be in one of the fridges across the far wall of the storage room. It should be labelled with "LyTBS".'

'Oh-okay. Yes, I can do that.' I begin to worry as I listen to his instructions. What if I mess up and get the wrong sample?

He stands and walks over to the bookcase that leans against the far wall. He rummages around through the books before turning back to me, a small piece of paper in his hands.

'I don't expect you'll be back, with or without my grandson...'

'Then why are you helping me?'

'I guess partially because I, like you, have nothing left to lose. But also, if you do by some miracle find him, I want you to give him a message.' He brings the paper over to the table and as he nears I can see it's a photo. On the back of it he draws a symbol I've never seen before.

'Here.' He passes me a small crinkled picture of a boy about my age. It's one of the generic shots we all have taken for our ARC user profiles. Across the back of the picture written in black pen is, 'Aiden, eighteen years old.' Under it is the strange design he's drawn: a vertical thick black line with a triangle hanging from the top.

I safely slide the picture into my pocket.

'Well, whatever your reason for helping me, thank you,' I say, standing up.

'Good luck,' he says. 'Something tells me you're going to need it.'

CHAPTER TWENTY-ONE

I wait until midnight before slipping out of bed and making my way to the Hospital Wing. The hallways are all dim with only the night-lights on and even the Atrium seems more ominous without its usual rush of people.

As I near the Hospital Wing, my eyes wander up to one of the screens that show the surface. The monitor is completely black. The sight of night up there has never bothered me before, but tonight it makes me worried. Would they really abandon the tainted on the surface?

When I get to the Hospital Wing it's eerily silent. Only the soft sound of my footsteps can be heard down the darkened hallway. The skin on the back of my neck prickles and my breath becomes short and shallow as I get closer to the entrance. When I reach the large swinging doors that lead inside I pause and take a nervous glance behind me. Only long dark shadows stretch across the corridor. No one knows I'm here.

A shot of adrenaline pulses through my body, urging me forward. I feel a sense of purpose, finally a sense of drive, of knowing what to do.

I push through the swinging doors to the entrance. Inside the overhead lights are all off and a lamp emitting a warm glow from on top of the reception counter overwhelms the faint blue hues of the lights skirting the floor. The entire waiting room is empty and the counter has been left unattended. Like all places in the ARC, the hospital runs on skeleton staff at night, so it's not surprising to find it so deserted.

I make my way across the reception and over to the slick metal doors of the elevator. I don't like the idea of getting in. In fact, I *hate* the idea of entering such a small space. The confines of elevators give me the jitters, but there aren't any stairwells close by and I'd rather not risk being caught wandering around.

The doors open with a loud 'ding,' causing me to jump back. My heart leaps with me and now feels like it's hammering from the base of my throat. I look around anxiously, but the sound doesn't seem to have alerted anyone.

The lift doors start to close and I dash forward to catch them. I hit the button for the third floor as I enter, and determinedly ignore the spike of fear that rushes through me as the doors close. I can feel a sheen of sweat developing on my forehead as I ascend. The space is just *so* small! When the doors reopen I lurch forward, away from the lift.

I don't care how far away the stairs are. I'm not going in that thing again.

As I approach the third floor nurses' station, I pause. The deserted station troubles me. I know fewer staff work at night, but where is everyone tonight?

I try to ignore the feeling and focus on where to go next. Several corridors lead off from the room and each one looks indistinguishable from the next. I pick at the hem of my sleeves as I try to think. I haven't been to the hospital enough times to remember where the storage rooms are. I'm not even certain I've been past the storage rooms before.

My stomach plummets, finding the storage rooms could take all night. I'm beginning to wish more than ever Quinn was here to help. She'd know exactly where we were going.

'*Idiot!*' I quietly swear at myself. I should've waited. I should've tried to talk to her again.

For a moment I think about turning back. Instead I find myself pacing forward. Quinn can be completely stubborn when she's made her mind up. There's no way she's helping me. Besides, I'm here now and I know I can do this.

I pick a hallway at random to begin my search. All along it are numbered doorways that have been left open. Inside I can see sleeping patients, their steady breaths only interrupted by the soft monotonous beeping of their monitors.

The passages are identical and I wander down them for what seems like eternity. Then finally I turn around a corner and spot a door up ahead with 'storage' written across the front of it.

Jackpot.

I have barely taken two steps towards the room though, when two nurses turn around the corner and start down the corridor towards me. They're both looking at the charts in their hands and talking, so they don't see me as I duck into the nearest room.

I stand just behind the door and listen as they pace closer. I look around the room for somewhere better to hide, but there aren't many options in here. It's bare except for the small cot that hosts a tiny girl who faintly wheezes in and out.

One of the women's voices sounds from just outside the door. I press my back harder into the wall and pray she doesn't come in here. It's dark, but not so dark that I'm invisible.

I listen to the women talking; they're so near I can clearly hear every word they say. *Please move on, please move on.* My body seizes up with shock as one of them pokes her head into the room to check on the girl. She's so close that if I reached my arm out I could touch her wispy grey locks of hair.

I clench my hands into little balls to stop them from shaking. If she turns even just a few inches to the right she'll see me.

'She's fine, I checked on her twenty minutes ago,' I hear the voice of the other nurse say.

'Oh I didn't realise. Isn't she a cutie?' The woman steps back out into the corridor and I finally start to breath normally again.

Once I'm certain the nurses have gone I go back into the corridor and finally make it to the storage room. I lightly place my hand on the door handle and briefly check over my shoulder to make sure no one is coming. Knowing the coast is clear I turn the handle, but it jars.

The door is locked.

Dammit.

I lean against the wall and glare down at the irritating door handle. I guess I should've expected they'd lock the room that stores all tainted blood samples. I'm surprised Dr. Wilson didn't warn me.

I should just go home and go to bed, but I know I won't do it; I've already made my mind up.

I slip back to the nurses' station I'd passed just a few minutes earlier. I glance around the room to make certain no one is here and then step behind the counter.

There are stacks of files placed upon the desk, all with patient names on them. I flick through the folders, but they're of no use to me. I shift them around the desk to make sure I haven't missed anything. There's nothing there.

I'm about to bend over to check the drawers under the table when I hear a heavy *clunk* coming from around the corner. I bolt up straight and stand dead still, listening. I wait, my heart pounding in my ears, my whole body frozen to the spot.

I can hear the low discreet hum of the lights, the long drawn out rasping of a patient trying to sleep, and the repetitive beeping of monitors. The unexpected noise doesn't return and after a minute of standing so still, not daring to even breathe, I slowly look around the corner and down the hallway. There's nothing there.

My heart still hammers as I turn back to the drawers and my hands shake as I try to ease the top one open.

It's stuck, so I carefully attempt to jiggle it to get it moving. With agonisingly slow movements it gradually begins to budge. As it wedges open further I see a ring of swipe cards. *Yes!*

It's hard to keep quiet as I sneak back towards the storage room. With the set of swipe cards in hand I'm too excited and I become careless, making too much noise as I walk. Despite this, I manage to make it back to the storage room without alerting anyone to my presence.

Now for the big problem: which one of these thirty swipe cards will open the door? I start to make my way through them one by one.

After trying half the cards on the ring I begin to feel doubtful. I start to lose hope that one of them will open the door. Who knows what they're even for? I swipe them through more urgently. This *has* to work. The key *has* to be on this ring. Each one that fails though, makes me feel less certain.

I'm almost to the end of the cards, when I swipe one through the reader and it finally lights up green with a small happy beep. The door handle smoothly turns. The door swings forward and I feel a wave of excitement when I see what's inside.

As the door opens wide my eyes fall on a room lined by glass doors that are frosted along the inside edge. The fridges are in here. Dr. Wilson was right.

I place my hand against the doorframe and lean into the room to see what the fridges hold. Those closest to the door look like they hold urine samples. But further down, against the back wall, there appears to be vials of blood. My heart skips a beat. I've found them.

I rush over to the fridges against the far wall, my whole body overwhelmed with anticipation. I've finally found a way to fake the blood test. The glass of the fridge door is all foggy but I can easily see the small tubes of blood sitting on the shelves inside. The frosty cold air from the fridge hits me as I wrench one of the doors back. I look on every shelf, but can't see any O-positive samples in this fridge. I go to the next one, and then the next. Finally, I open a fridge that contains samples labelled 'LyTBS: O+'. I grab the first sample I can get my hands on and slip it in the pocket of my pants.

I let out a breath of relief. I'd been so worried the samples wouldn't be here and this would all be for nothing. I close the fridge door and go to turn around, but just as I move to leave, I feel the sickening touch of a hand firmly taking grip of my shoulder.

A chill runs down my spine as the strong, secure grasp of the hand spins me around.

The fierce, menacing eyes of an official are trained down upon me.

'What are you doing in here?' he spits at me, his words quick and harsh.

'I... I....'

He grabs my arm and tugs me to the doorway and out into the hall. 'Oh you're going to be in trouble for this,' he says darkly.

As he turns to close the door, his grip on my arm lessens slightly and in a blind panic I rip my arm free from his grasp and begin to run.

'GET BACK HERE!' he roars from behind me.

But I'm off. I tear around the corner and find myself back at the nurses' station. I don't know which way to go, but his footsteps sound from right behind me.

He yells loudly into his CommuCuff, 'Third floor, Hospital Wing...'

Without any thought other than escape I run past the nurses' station and off down a passageway. Careering around the corner I bowl over a nurse and her folder spills from her hands, sending the papers inside flying everywhere.

'Sorry!' I yell, as I attempt to regain my footing and stumble past her.

My heart thuds loudly in my ears and I can hear myself panting for breath as I turn down another endless corridor. My legs are burning from the exertion and my head is beginning to feel faint.

I check over my shoulder as I turn around the corner. The official is still there, but is beginning to fall behind. I push myself to run faster, clenching my teeth as pain shoots through my legs. I know I need to escape. I can't be caught.

I whip around another corner and select a patient's room at random, diving into it before the official can catch me up and see where I've gone.

A man sleeps on the bed inside and I can hear a heavy snore coming from him as he rasps in and out. I'm concerned he might hear me, wake up, and sound the alarm, but I don't have a choice. I scramble towards him, duck down and crawl under his bed.

I lie flat against the ground, with one hand securely wrapped around the vial in my pocket and my eyes focused on the doorway, which I can see through the small gap between the floor and the blanket that reaches down to it. My chest heaves, exhausted from running, and somehow I manage to keep my panting quiet.

In the distance I can hear the official's pounding footsteps. They're faint at first, but slowly they get louder and louder. I want to close my eyes, to pretend this isn't happening.

His footsteps slow as he nears the room I'm in. I begin to tremble with nerves. Does he somehow know I'm in here? His voice yells out and I draw back in shock. He's closer than I'd thought.

'She's got away...'

I raise my head off the floor to try and hear better. There's the muffled sound of a response, but it isn't clear enough to make out. He must be on his cuff.

'Yeah, we'll get her,' he says, before I hear the distinct beep of a comm disengaging. For a moment there's total silence, then comes the sound of his footsteps retreating back in the direction he just came.

I close my eyes and try to get my body to relax. He's gone. But he'd sounded sure he'd fine me. Could he know who I am?

I wait under the bed for almost half an hour before I make my way out from beneath it. I carefully steal my way back across the ARC; stopping before every corner and slowing whenever I see someone coming towards me in the distance. I feel quite certain there's an alert out for me now. If an official sees me out here in the middle of the night, they'll easily be able to tell I'm the one they're after.

I only start to feel slightly less worried when I get closer to home. As I turn down my corridor I feel a giddy relief to see the flickering light bulb over my doorway. I'm finally safe.

I hurry towards the door, eager to get inside. I swipe my key card against the lock, and the sensor lights up green. I'm home.

I go to turn the door handle, except it turns of its own accord and opens to show Quinn standing in the doorway. Her face looks grave. She's clearly still pissed at me.

'Hi,' I say, awkwardly. I don't really know what to say to her to make things better. I'm surprised she's even looking at me directly.

'I'm so sorry,' she mouths. I frown at her, confused, what is she...

The door opens fully to reveal two officials standing there in wait.

They both step past Quinn towards me. 'Elle Winters, you need to come with us.'

'What?' I take an involuntary step back towards the opposite wall.

Without breaking stride, the first official grabs me by the arm and pulls me back down the hallway.

'What's going on?' I ask him, fear pulsing through my body. How did they know who I am? How did they find me? I turn back to Quinn who has followed us out. She stands just outside our doorway watching silently as the two men escort me away.

'Quinn!' I yell at her for help.

She runs to catch up with us. 'Don't worry Elle, I know what to do. I can fix this!' she says, clambering to keep up. I glance up at the two officials, who walk either side of me. Without a second to lose, I dig my free hand down into the pocket of my pants and pull the vial of blood out. I launch myself away from the official who grips my arm so tightly, yelping in pain as his fingers drag against my skin.

Though his fingers grasp to maintain their hold on me I manage to shake him loose. I throw my arms around Quinn. 'Please *help* me,'

I beg, slipping the vial into her pocket, not giving her any choice but to take it.

As it slides safely into her pocket she pulls back from me and glances down, her hand diving into the pocket to feel what I've given her. Her whole body freezes as her hand wraps around the vial.

Before I can see she understands I need her to keep the vial safe for me, two strong hands wrap their way around my waist and my body jerks back, away from Quinn. 'What do you think you're doing?'

I try to turn to respond to the official, but my face is flung in the other direction as one of the men slaps me.

'Don't do that again!' he roars down at me. My cheek burns intensely and tears sting in the corners of my eyes. I reach up to place my hand against the tender spot, but the officials grab my wrists and I'm yanked back into a walk.

It's not till we near the end of the corridor that I find the courage to turn and look at Quinn. She still stands frozen to the same spot, transfixed on the vial clenched tightly in her hand. She slowly looks up at me, her green eyes filled with fear.

The official tugs me around a corner and I lose sight of Quinn and the vial of blood. My one chance, my one hope, is with the one person who has refused to help me.

Quinn had said she knew what to do, that she could fix this. Only problem is, tucked away safely in remand is exactly where she'll want me to be.

CHAPTER TWENTY-TWO

I try to ignore my surroundings, but that's hard to do when you're in the cold, white confines of a tiny cell. There's barely enough room for the metal bunk bed that looms over the small table I sit at, and a red flickering eye watches me constantly from above.

The mirrored wall in front of me reflects the image of a girl I don't know. Her hair is a mess, her cheeks sag with exhaustion and her blue eyes are heavy with despair. I turn away from the vision, unable to look at it any longer. God, I look atrocious.

The metal leg of my chair squeals as I shuffle it closer to the table so I can lay my head down on my arms. This place is so small. I close my eyes and try to keep calm. *Too small* for my liking. It's barely three meters square.

I take a deep breath in and then out, and try to avoid thinking about how confined the space is. I can't let it get to me.

It's not hard to distract myself with thoughts of how absolutely screwed I am running through my mind. While I haven't been told what's going to happen to me yet, I know it can't be anything good.

What was I thinking? I should've given up when I found the door locked. I probably shouldn't have gone in the first place. I grimace as I remember being caught.

An official walks into the room carrying a glass of water for me. His presence is a reprieve from my inescapable dark thoughts.

'Thank you,' I say, taking the glass and drinking up the contents.

'That's okay,' he replies. 'I thought I should come in and update you. We've booked you in for a hearing before Counsellor Jeffries at eleven o'clock this morning.' I gulp in response and my tired eyes look down at my empty wrist to check the current time. I rub the bare skin where my CommuCuff usually resides. Only an official or a doctor can remove it from you and I feel so naked without it. I wish mine hadn't been confiscated.

'I suggest you be completely truthful with him about the night's events,' he continues. 'Jeffries doesn't take dishonesty lightly.' I nod back at him. 'We realise you don't have a guardian, so we have contacted Quinn Roberts. We'll let her in once she gets here.' He turns abruptly and leaves.

It feels like I wait forever for Quinn to arrive. Time seems to drag in this shoebox of a room. When Quinn finally enters she rushes over and hugs me, once the door shuts firmly behind her.

'I came as quickly as I could,' she says, as she takes a seat next to me at the table. 'What were you thinking Elle? Breaking into a storage room of all places?'

'I'm sorry, I was being stupid, and you weren't talking to me...' Stupid seems like an understatement. 'What have you done with the...' My voice trails off as I catch my reflection in the mirrored wall again. Someone could easily be listening to what I say. I can't mention the blood sample.

Quinn seems to have caught on though and is slowly shaking her head.

'I've dealt with it,' she says quietly. The meaning behind her words is clear. She's gotten rid of the sample.

I sink down in my chair.

'You can't be worrying about that now,' Quinn says. 'You've got a merciless councilman waiting for you. You need to focus on getting through your hearing.'

'Jeffries,' I groan.

'It will be fine. Just pass it off as a silly prank, or a dare, and I'll sort the rest out.'

She sits there so calmly and I feel a rush of gratitude. I'm so incredibly relieved she's here to help me. Maybe some time in remand is worth it if it means she's talking to me again?

When the official walks back into the room, I instinctively recoil back.

'It's time to go,' he says.

I'm escorted to a large room towards the back of the official offices. Several people are already seated, quietly chatting to each other. There are two desks in the middle of the room, and several rows of chairs toward the back. Down the other end is a long, elevated table that runs the width of the room.

I'm led to a chair in the front row and asked to sit—like I have a choice. I quietly obey and Quinn follows, sitting beside me.

The whole atmosphere in the room changes when Counsellor Jeffries enters. As he walks in, his long black gown billowing around him, everyone in the room falls silent and stands. The councilman takes long commanding strides over to the seat in the middle of the elevated table at the front. As he sits, so does everyone else.

He's old, maybe in his seventies, and his face is withered and sharp. He doesn't look sympathetic at all. My stomach clenches with nerves and I can barely concentrate on what is being said as the official stands and lays out the charges against me.

Jeffries' eyes seem to slice right through me and I wince in response. I bet this guy can sniff a lie from a mile away.

'Miss Winters,' he says. 'What do you have to say for yourself?'

I stand and slowly approach the closest desk. My palms are sweaty and my hands shake with nerves.

'I did what the officer alleges,' I say, my voice quiet and full of remorse. 'I was at the hospital and I took some swipe cards to break into the storage room. It was a silly prank, and I am extremely apologetic for my actions.' I sit down as quickly as I can and allow myself to slowly exhale.

I've barely taken a seat when Quinn springs up. 'Please excuse my rude interruption Sir. My name is Quinn Roberts. Elle is a minor and I'm the adult who takes responsibility for her. There are a few things I would like to bring to your attention.' He nods to Quinn as if to say, 'Go on.'

'Thank you. First off I would like to provide you with some character references from her teachers at school.' She walks up to the table he sits at and passes them to him, before returning back to her place alongside me.

'These references outline that this was completely out of character for Elle. She is a good student, and would under normal circumstances never act in such a careless manner. I would also like to point out that her best friend was taken last week, and another girl the week before. She, herself, has her testing on Monday. This situation she is in is very out of the ordinary, and has made her unusually distressed, causing her to act out in such an uncharacteristic manner.'

'Thank you Miss Roberts,' Jeffries says.

He inclines his head towards Quinn indicating she should sit. As Quinn slides down into the seat next to me I notice my jaw has reflexively opened wide with surprise. I had no idea how much she knew about this stuff. I glance up at the councilman who is reading through the references, and then lean my mouth close to her ear.

'How did you know all that?' I whisper with awe.

She merely shrugs in response like it's no big deal.

The councilman clears his throat. 'In light of the information provided to me,' he says, 'I would tend to agree with what Miss Roberts has said. I am inclined to believe this action was out of character for Miss Winters. I do find it strange she would break into a hospital storage room and I look upon this act with a degree of suspicion. This is a first time offence for Miss Winters, so I will treat it accordingly.

'Miss Winters,' he says, looking directly at me. 'I will order that you undertake an extra five hours of community service for each week of the following month. Furthermore, you will remain in remand until the time of your testing on Monday so you can reflect upon what you have done.' He closes the file on his table and another official stands to begin announcing the next case.

My eyes dart to Quinn, who looks at me, relieved. *Relieved?* How can she be relieved? I can't be imprisoned for the weekend. I won't have a chance of finding a way to be taken from inside a cell. This is exactly what she wants. What the hell am I going to do?

An official takes a hold of my arm and escorts me towards the door.

'This way,' he indicates, once out in the hallway. Quinn goes to follow, but he stops her. 'You can't come any further.'

'I just wanted to say goodbye...' she pleads. He looks at her blankly before turning and pulling me along behind him.

'It's going to be okay!' Quinn calls out to me. I refuse to turn and acknowledge it though. She must be so happy I'm safely locked away, unable to get myself into any more trouble. I can practically hear the glee in her voice.

Once I'm placed back in my cell the door swings closed with a short, abrupt *clunk*. As I hear the noise my heart sinks. I'm officially a prisoner, and now any chance I had at trying to find my way to Sebastian is completely lost.

IT'S AMAZING how draining being stuck in a cell can be. My life has quickly become the weary monotony of staring at a wall. For countless hours I am a statue, and it's completely exhausting. I have no idea how I've made it through two days of this.

Officials come and go with food and water, but it's a small reprieve from the desolate isolation in here.

Around dinner my stomach starts growling. As if on cue an official walks in with a tray. It's the same official that has been bringing me meals over the last few days. He's the first one I've ever encountered who doesn't seem completely uptight, in fact he's almost friendly.

'How are you holding up?' he asks kindly, as he places the tray down on the end of my bed.

'I'm okay thanks,' I say. I sit up on the bed, bending my head slightly so it doesn't touch the bunk above. 'Can't say these will go down as the best days in my life.'

'No, I can't imagine they would. Just one more sleep now.' He says it to cheer me up, but the words have the reverse effect. I can feel the colour drain away from my face. My testing is tomorrow.

'Could be worse though,' he continues. 'You think this is bad?' He waves his hand around the room. 'You should've seen what they used to do for punishment. Makes a few days in here look like a holiday.' He shakes his head at the memory, disapprovingly.

'They haven't always just used these cells?'

'Cells? No, these used to be living quarters.'

'What happened?' I ask, intrigued and somewhat glad these are no longer used to house people. I don't think I could handle living in a room this small.

'Well, when we all first came to the ARC, it was jam-packed. Especially after the Old Wing was rendered unstable. They had to use every spare space to fit in all the refugees they could. We were almost lucky people began getting taken. It certainly freed up more living space, that's for sure.'

'So what happened to offenders?'

'Ah, bit of a messy subject that one really. Mostly they just increased community service hours. Slap across the wrist type of punishment.' He looks slightly uncomfortable, like he regrets bringing the topic up. His eyes keep darting back to the door.

'What about the bad offenders?' I persevere.

He looks around, like someone might hear him and in a hushed voice says, 'Well it got to the point where they didn't really have much of a choice with some people. They had to send a few of the bad ones to the surface.'

'They gave them a death sentence?' I ask, horrified.

He shrugs. 'Like I said, your sentence is practically a holiday. Anyway, it's not for you to worry. You'll be out in the morning.' He leaves me to eat my dinner.

I push the meal they have provided away from me. I can't eat, and I'm not sure if I'll be able to sleep tonight either. After what the official has said about how easily they would toss out the bad offenders, I have a foreboding feeling the Council wouldn't have any qualms dealing with the tainted in much the same way.

CHAPTER TWENTY-THREE

When I wake in the morning my mind is confused. My thoughts are tangled and the terrors that crept into my fitful sleep linger on the edge of my consciousness. I open my eyes and stare at the stark white walls of the tiny room.

I can't shake the chills brought on by the nightmares that haunted me last night. I gather up the bed sheet and clutch it to my chest, trying to quell the fears caused by my dreams, and subdue the nerves that have begun to tremor in my gut.

The door opens abruptly and a man in official white walks in.

'Time to go,' he says shortly. I nod and stagger out of the bed to follow him. He leads me out into the hallway and as I walk behind him I drowsily thread my fingers through my hair in an attempt to flatten it into place. When we reach the main office the official passes me my CommuCuff back and watches to make sure I fix it properly back onto my wrist.

Once he's satisfied my cuff is fastened he passes me my necklace and the picture Dr. Wilson had given me of his grandson, Aiden. The photo had been in my pocket on arrival and they'd taken it along with my cuff and necklace. I look at the boy's face on the paper and then angrily shove the picture back into my pocket, not caring if it crinkles. The doctor had been *supposed* to help me, not get me thrown in remand.

The official leads me through a security door. As soon as the door opens I immediately spot Quinn across the other side of the room. She's in the middle of chatting animatedly with one of the officials, and as I approach I hear her say, 'Yes. I'll be taking her over to her testing now.' My stomach does a small flip as I hear the word 'testing'. It's unbelievable how quickly this day's arrived.

Quinn looks at me when I stop beside her. The reserved purse of her lips and distance in her eyes reveal she's being careful not to show any true emotion. As soon as we're out of the official offices the façade drops.

'So what made you think to go to the storage rooms?' she asks, lowering her voice.

'One of the patients in the Aged Care Ward used to be a doctor. He did a lot of work with the tainted and told me I could get a tainted blood sample from there,' I respond, lowering my voice as well.

'You told him what you want to do?' she asks, concerned.

I shrug. 'He's got as much reason to hate people being taken as I do and I trust him.'

'Okay...' she says, obviously unconvinced. She looks up and down the empty hallway swiftly, and then grabs my arm to stop me.

'Here,' she whispers, as she slips something into my hand. I look down and see the vial of blood.

'I thought you didn't want to help?' I say, confused.

'What I said the other night ... I was upset and worried. I freaked out. Then, when that official took you, I realised I can't protect you from everything. Besides, I know how important this is to you. I'm just sorry I didn't come around sooner.'

I smile at her warmly. I'd lost all hope I could really pull this off. 'But after what you said in the cell, I thought you'd destroyed the sample...'

Quinn shakes her head. 'No, what I actually did was get a new label for it and one of the proper specimen containers to hold it in. You can't just leave a blood sample out in the open all weekend. What were you thinking?'

She looks so disapproving about my lack of knowledge on sample storage that I laugh. But for some reason the laugh only makes me feel sad and I can feel tears glistening in my eyes. I look away to make sure Quinn doesn't notice.

'Listen we don't have long. How are you planning on swapping the vials?' she asks, as I turn back to her.

'I—I hadn't really thought about it,' I say, panic touching my voice as it begins to set in. I'm acutely aware of how close to my testing it is. How little time I have left until I give up everything I've ever known to follow through with this plan.

Quinn shrugs at me in response. 'Wing it, I'm sure you'll think of something.' I look at her incredulously. 'Well you know what I mean. You're going to have to use your initiative. I'm sure you'll be fine.'

'Yeah, okay,' I say with complete uncertainty, my hand quivering as I slip the vial of blood into my pocket.

'It's going to work.'

'We'll see,' I mumble. I hear footsteps coming around the corner and half-turn to see an official walking towards us. Quinn nods her head to the side, indicating we should continue moving.

We walk at a leisurely pace, but all too soon I find we're at the hospital. Quinn stops before we enter and hugs me.

'Everything is going to be fine,' she whispers in my ear. She pulls back and looks at me. 'Any second thoughts? It's not too late to back out you know.'

I shake my head, adrenaline beginning to strengthen my resolve. 'Sebastian would do it for me,' I respond.

'I know,' she says, rubbing my arm reassuringly. She peers down at her CommuCuff. 'We're a bit early.'

'Let's just get this over with,' I say, sounding braver than I feel.

'After you...' She indicates with her arm towards the door.

I push open the door and walk to the reception counter. The woman peers up at me expectantly.

'Hi, I'm Elle Winters. I'm here for my testing.' The woman looks over at her computer screen.

'Take a seat. The doctor's running about five minutes behind,' she says. I follow Quinn over to the waiting room seats. I'm shaking, my stomach rolls with nausea and I can feel beads of sweat building on my forehead.

'I don't feel so good,' I whisper to Quinn. She takes a hold of my hand, squeezing it firmly.

'It's going to be okay,' she whispers back. Her face is completely drained of colour though. She's just as nervous as I am. I feel my way into my pocket with my fingers and firmly clasp them around the vial. I need to keep it safe.

'What if something goes wrong? What if it goes right and I never see you again?' I say, my words so quick and quiet I'm not certain Quinn will hear them correctly.

She catches my eye, and looking at me directly she replies, 'Elle, you are so incredibly smart and strong. *When* we are separated I know you have the fight and the determination to carry on. Your priority is to keep yourself safe and find Sebastian. And don't worry about me. I don't think this is the end for us. We'll see each other again, just maybe not as soon as we'd like.' She smiles sadly as she says this.

I go to look down but she takes a hold of my chin and lifts it, forcing my eyes back to hers. 'Seriously Elle, promise me you'll take care of yourself.'

'I promise,' I choke out in barely a whisper. Why does this feel like goodbye?

'Elle Winters?' a man in a long white lab coat announces, as he peers up from his clipboard.

'I love you Elle.'

'I love you too Quinn.' We hug each other tightly.

'Elle Winters?' The man repeats louder.

'Everything will be fine,' Quinn says determinedly. I nod in response. Then, taking a deep breath, I turn around and walk over to the man. I don't look back at Quinn—I can't look back. If I do, I know the vial of blood will stay firmly put in my pocket and I'll let this opportunity go.

'Your cuff.' The man holds his hand out expectantly. I reach out my arm and he takes my CommuCuff in his hand. He swipes a card over the face of it and with a *click* it unlocks and he pulls it from my wrist. I've already spent the weekend without it and it's surprisingly hard to hand it over again so soon. I rub my bare wrist uncomfortably.

'This way.' The man leads me down several corridors and stops in front of 'Exam Room 2.' He opens the door and ushers me inside.

Exam Room 2 is just like every other exam room I've been tested in. It's utterly devoid of any colour and entirely sterile looking. Large white tiles cover the room from floor to ceiling and everything in here is so clean it sparkles.

On one side of the room there's a long metal bench and a wash-basin. The bench gleams under the bright lights, which bounce off its cold steel surface and the array of glass beakers that cover it. An old and obsolete looking computer whirs from the corner of the room and it's hooked up to some sort of microscope.

Across the other side of the room is the exam table. It is covered in blue material with white wax paper running along the centre of it. It butts up against a thin metal cabinet of drawers, the top of which has a series of bean-shaped metal dishes. Then, in the far corner, hangs a long, white curtain that has been drawn for patients to change behind.

'Please take a seat on the bed,' the man says behind me. 'The doctor will be with you shortly.' I take a step forward and the door shuts behind me.

I've barely sat down when the door swings back open and a woman enters. She takes her glasses out of her pocket, puts them up to her eyes and looks down at her chart. This woman is all business.

'Elle Winters I presume?'

I nod in response. I'm not certain I can say anything right now. *One breath in, one breath out.* The woman barely acknowledges me, but that one glance is all I need to see she is cold and calculating.

'I'm Doctor Patel. I will be administering your test today.' She takes a stool out from under the bench and brings it over to sit by me.

'Could you tell me how you've been feeling lately?'

'Mostly fine,' I say quietly. She nods and starts writing on her clipboard. 'But this weekend I haven't been too well.'

'Go on...' She looks up, curious.

'Well, I've had aches and pains, and been feeling really hot and sweaty.' She's back writing furiously on her sheet again.

'Anything else?'

'Um, not that I can think of.'

'And you didn't think to come to the hospital if you were feeling ill? You should be aware of the fever protocols in place.'

'Oh, I've been in remand all weekend. I didn't really think it was an option.'

'I see.' Once she finishes writing she puts her pen down on the clipboard and then places them on her stool. She walks over to the cabinet next to me and rummages through its drawers, which squeak and rattle as she opens and closes them. She seems to be taking various items out of each one and then placing them on one of the silver trays that sit on top of the cabinet. The glint of a needle catches my eye as she places it on the tray. This is really happening.

Picking a tourniquet up off the tray, the doctor proceeds to tie it around my upper arm before pulling it tight. I begin to feel clammy and beads of sweat slowly trickle down the back of my neck.

'Okay Elle, this is just going to be a small prick,' she says. I swear there's an evil glint in her eye and her lips are pulled back in a way that makes her look slightly crazed as she lowers the needle closer.

I feel a pinch in my elbow crease as she jabs the needle into my arm. I suck a quick breath in through my teeth and watch as the blood slowly trickles out into the vial. *Wow, there's a lot of blood in there.*

After what seems like an eternity, she pulls the needle out and removes the vial placing them both on the silver tray. I watch the small glass vial intently. It seems so close, but at the same time so impossibly far away. How am I supposed to swap it with the vial in my pocket without the doctor noticing?

I watch her and the vial carefully, waiting for an opportune moment to make the swap. But I don't know what to do. She's hovering by the cabinet and there's no way I can make my move while she's still in such close proximity.

I begin to feel lightheaded and I try to ignore it. *It was just a little blood*, I remind myself. I can't be distracted right now. The doctor picks up the vial and takes a pen out of her pocket to write on its small white label.

Shit.

I feel a sudden, overwhelming panic crash through me. I can't let her write on that vial. I watch the pen get closer to the vial and the panic surges through me stronger. Having no idea what to do, and in a fit of desperation, I resort to theatrics.

'Agh,' I stand up and moan, staggering into her and lightly grabbing her arm. She places the pen and the vial back on the tray. I try not to grin in satisfaction.

'Elle are you okay?' She places her hand against my forehead.

'I really don't feel too good,' I whimper. I don't even have to fake it. Between stress and having my blood taken I legitimately feel woozy.

'Okay, just sit back down.' She helps me back on the bed. I make sure I sit right at the end of it. The vial is now easily within my reach.

The doctor takes a towel out of the cabinet. 'You're really hot Elle, I'm just going to wet this and we'll put it on your head which should hopefully make you feel a bit better.' She turns and walks to the sink.

Now's my chance.

I hear the gush of water rushing out of the tap. Ever so quickly, I grab the vial out of my pocket and go to swap it for the one on the table. With the two vials next to each other my mouth involuntarily drops open.

The caps on the vials are different colours.

Crap!

The one Quinn gave me has a red lid and the vial with my blood in it has a yellow lid. I hear her switching the tap off. *Screw it.* I grab the vial with the yellow lid and place it in my pocket, leaving the other in its place.

If I wasn't sweating before, I definitely am now. She turns to me and walks over, completely unaware of the switch.

'You can lie down if you like?'

'No it's okay, I'm happy to sit.' She passes me the wet towel. I quietly dab my forehead with it as she goes back to writing on the vial.

As she picks the vial up she seems confused. I groan out aloud causing her to look back at me.

'How are you feeling? Are you sure you don't want to lie down?'

'No I'm okay.'

'Is the wet towel helping?'

'Yes. Thank you.' She nods and turns back to the vial. Then, without another thought, she writes my details down on the label.

'Okay, wait here. I'm going to take this to get it tested. Shouldn't be too long.' She walks out the door with the vial in hand.

I exhale loudly as she exits. I hadn't even realised I'd been holding my breath. It worked and I can't believe it. I managed to swap the vials over. I quickly jump off the bench and rush over to the sink to empty the vial I can feel burning a hole in my pocket.

As I wash away the evidence though, it dawns on me.

It worked and I'm about to be taken.

CHAPTER TWENTY-FOUR

The coldness of the room seeps into my bones as I wait. My eyes are trained on the door waiting for the doctor to return with the news I already know is coming. I curl my knees up to my chest and hug them close to my body. The whole idea of being taken to rescue Sebastian had been so romantic, heroic even, at the time. But now, faced with the reality of leaving, I'm not certain I can go through with it.

I've been waiting in the room for half an hour when Dr. Patel re-enters. The hairs on the back of my neck stand on end and I hold my pendant in my hand tightly. The thought I've been trying to avoid thinking for the last half-hour surfaces to the forefront of my mind. *I don't want to be taken.*

Dr. Patel looks down at the chart in her hands, taking her time as she reads through the results.

'So, I've got good news,' she says reassuringly. 'Your test came back all clear.'

I stare at her blankly in response.

'That means you're not tainted,' she explains.

Again I don't respond and she looks at me like I'm slow in the head.

'What?' I finally ask, incredulity evident in the tone of my voice.

'You're fine dear.'

'Really?' I say, in a manner more accusatory than questioning. She looks slightly confused, but checks her chart again.

'Yes, really.' She gives an awkward laugh.

She seems confused by my response. Admittedly, I am acting like a crazy person. She does appear genuinely sincere about my results though. They must've come back clear. Maybe I grabbed the wrong sample?

My whole body relaxes as I accept the news. I can't believe how paranoid I am. I'd almost started an interrogation of this poor doctor. I vaguely shake my head at my own stupidity.

I've barely relaxed when my chest contracts abruptly. My whole being becomes entirely consumed with guilt and I feel like I can barely breathe. I'm unquestionably the most horrible, selfish person ever. I can't believe that, for even a second, I could be happy I'm not tainted. That I could be happy when I will never see Sebastian again.

I sadly clutch my hand to my chest as I think of the face I will never see again, the laughs we will never share and the things I will never be able to tell him.

'So can I go then?' I ask, absently, I need to get away from this room. I want more than anything to be alone right now.

'Not quite yet,' she says. 'I'm concerned about the symptoms you were describing to me from over the weekend. I would like to do just a couple more tests. They shouldn't take too long.'

'Oh, okay,' I murmur, my voice unmistakably disappointed. I've been in the stark white confines of this room for so long now. Plus, I've been locked up all weekend. I just want to go back to my own quarters.

'If you wouldn't mind getting up and following me? I haven't got the right instruments in here so we'll have to go to my office.' I stand up and take a step towards the door.

'No, this way.' She directs me towards the back of the room. 'My office is just back here.' I follow her to the changing curtain, which she yanks back. There is nothing there except the plain white wall of the testing room. She moves forward and presses against one of the large wall panels, which opens with a *pop*. She pulls it back into her and indicates for me to go through first.

Her whole body is rigid and her eyes are blank as I walk past her and through the open panel. As soon as I enter I hear the door slam shut behind me and I'm immediately engulfed in complete darkness.

'Hello? Dr. Patel?' I call out nervously. 'What's going on?' There's no response to my questions, only silence. My body starts shaking. It's so incredibly dark in here.

'Anyone?' I yell out. A light flicks on overhead. I'm in a small box of a room that you could barely fit four people in. *Deep breaths, long deep breaths,* I think. But I can't get control of my breathing. My chest feels constricted and my lungs refuse to take in more than a short breath of air. I hold my hand firmly against my chest. I feel like I'm drowning and unable to come up for air.

I turn back to the wall panel I entered through and start pressing my hands against it, trying to open it up.

'C'mon, c'mon...' I quickly give up on pushing and start shoving my body against the panel.

The room shudders and I throw my hands against the walls to steady myself. *What the hell is happening?* The room begins to move and my stomach surges with the motion. I'm not in a room, but an elevator.

'Quinn,' I say with a whisper, as I think of her sitting down in the waiting room.

There has to be an exit in here!

'Quinn?' I yell, my whole body wrenching around as I try to find a way to make it stop. I pat along the walls, looking for some secret way out of here. But nothing is in here, just the constant hum as the lift makes its quick ascent.

'Quinn?' I scream, as I punch my fists against the wall.

'Quinn!' I scream louder. I shout her name over and over again.

The elevator shudders to a stop and silence takes over. A few seconds later one of the walls retracts. I shrink back into the corner of the space as a large man dressed in black comes to stand at the entrance.

'This way,' he growls. I don't move. He roughly grabs my arm and pulls me out of the lift and into a hallway.

'What's going on? Where are you taking me?' My voice quivers with emotion. He doesn't respond.

'Please,' my voice breaks, 'please tell me where we're going?' He opens a door and shoves me inside another dark room. The door slams shut as I topple inside. I run back to the door and bang on it.

'Hey! You can't just leave me in here!' I yell at him. I slam my fists against the door harder. 'Hey!' I call out louder.

'He can't help you.' A woman's voice comes from behind me. I jump and turn. I hadn't realised anyone was in here. The light comes on overhead and a lady in a black suit stands just inside another entranceway. Her dark hair is pulled back harshly in a tight bun giving her face unforgiving lines. Her whole stance exudes authority.

'Elle, my name is Maggie. Take a seat,' she says. I take small, cautious steps towards her. The room is comfortable looking, but foreign to anything I've experienced in the ARC.

The walls are painted a rich golden colour and along the roof are exposed wooden beams. The floor is covered in a thick plush carpet that is so inviting I'd probably want to roll in it if I wasn't so traumatised. Elaborate paintings hang in heavy, intricate frames from the walls and cosy couches are arranged in a circle around a rich wooden coffee table that looks onto a fireplace.

She directs me to sit at one of the couches and nervously I take a seat.

'Would you like something to drink Elle?' I shake my head and turn away from her, trying to compose myself. My whole body is still shaking and my breath continues to catch in my throat.

I allow my eyes to settle on the fireplace. The fire is so vibrant and bright, and it makes the softest little crackling noises. It's the first time I've seen one in real life and I could probably watch the flames all day as they flicker and dance playfully.

'Now I know the last few minutes have been very stressful. I want to apologise for any worry or discomfort that you may have felt. I'm about to tell you a few things and I want you to listen to everything I have to say before commenting. Okay?'

I nod to show I understand. I'm not certain I trust my voice to be steady right now.

'Okay. Now this may come as a shock to you, but your blood result has come back indicating you are tainted.' I'd thought as much, especially given my terrifying exit from the doctor's office. I can't imagine them doing this if all I'd had was a cold.

'Unfortunately,' she continues. 'The best way we've found of taking people out of the ARC is by using the method we've applied to you. We realise it's scary, and unfair, but it's the only way we can get people out without affecting life down in the ARC.'

'What's going to happen to me?' The words rush out and the daggered look she gives me makes me immediately regret saying them.

'I'm getting to that,' she snaps, her lips tightening and her cold steely eyes hardening. She clears her throat and looks down to dust her skirt before continuing. When she looks up the coldness in her eyes has lessened.

'Firstly, we are going to allow you to record a video to say goodbye to your friends and family. It is of the utmost importance you do not describe any of what has happened to you. Otherwise we shall not be passing it along, and you will not get to say your goodbyes. Before making this video I need to explain to you that it is in your family and friend's best interests if you tell them not to worry and not to come after you.

'Any kind of agitation on the part of a friend or family member will be met with restraint of the individual, imprisonment or, in some cases, them being taken to the *surface*. I can assure you, if that happens, they will not survive.' She looks at me sternly. This woman is not kidding; she means every word of what she says.

I gulp, and nod my head. She stands stiffly and walks towards the door she must have entered through at the back of the room.

'Follow me,' she says firmly. I jump up and walk over to her. I can't imagine anyone refusing. This woman is vicious and as much as I'm worried about where I'm going, I think I'm more frightened of staying here with her.

She takes me through to the desolate grey room I recognise from Sebastian's recording. Sitting in the middle of the room is a video camera on a tripod facing a chair. The camera is hooked up to a computer sitting on the table next to it.

Maggie directs me to sit on the chair, so I quickly follow her instructions. I sit up straight and look up into the eye of a camera. I must look a mess. How will footage of me looking so obviously distressed reassure Quinn?

'I recommend you direct your video to one person. It's usually easiest that way,' she says, as she plays around with the video camera.

'Do you know who you want the video to go to?' she asks.

'Quinn Roberts,' I murmur. 'I live with her.' She nods and a little red light appears on the front of the camera.

I grip the edges of my chair and wonder where Quinn is right now. Would she still be in the waiting room? I imagine her sitting there, hoping I might return. Tears sting my eyes and I choke them back down.

I tighten my grip on the cold metal chair. I feel like such an idiot. How did I not realise my results had come back *tainted* when she revealed the secret doorway? It was so obvious! Even before then I should've known.

The red light on the camera goes off.

'Elle,' Maggie says. 'Are you going to do a recording?'

'Sorry. Yes. I was just trying to think what to say.'

'Okay, are you ready now?'

'I think so.' The red light flicks on again.

Here goes nothing.

'Quinn. I'm so sorry I'm going away. Who would've thought that when I entered that room I wouldn't be coming back out again?'

I look over at Maggie who nods for me to continue.

'You've been the best friend I could ever wish for. The best *family* I could ever wish for. You have been my guardian angel. You taught me to stand up for myself. But more than that, you always stood up for me when I didn't know how. I will never be able to repay you for looking after me the way you have.' I can feel tears welling in my eyes.

'I'm going to miss you like you wouldn't believe. I want you to be so happy and to continue living your life just as we did before. I'm going to be fine, so I don't want you to worry. Please say goodbye to everyone for me. I love you so much. Stay safe.'

Tears stream down my face as Maggie turns the camera off. I feel like I've traded Sebastian for Quinn. I'd been so caught up in the idea of rescuing Sebastian I hadn't anticipated losing her. I never intended for this to be a choice between the two of them. I was so wrong. And now, recording this video, I feel like I've had to say my final goodbye.

'What now?' I ask, a hint of apprehension seeping into my voice.

She ignores my question and bends down over the computer monitor. After a minute of her staring at the screen she stands.

'Follow me,' she orders.

I silently follow the woman down hallway after hallway. Her heels clip clop along the hard floor as we walk. We reach a dead end and she presses a button on the wall, which lights up to the touch.

Doors slide open in front of us and I have to stop myself from whimpering out loud. Another elevator. I've always avoided them like the plague and I'm already on a second for the day. But for once, my fear of the tiny space is overcome by my dread of where it's taking me.

I make my way into it and clutch my hands against the walls. It shudders to life causing my stomach to lurch again. I can feel the steady momentum of the lift moving upwards and I try not to think about its destination. But it's unavoidable. The lift is going up so visions of the ravaged surface plague the forefront of my mind.

Before I know it, the doors slide open again and we step out.

We're in a large bright room. Actually large is an understatement, and I doubt 'room' is the appropriate word to describe the enormous expanse I find myself in. It's *huge*, bigger even than the plantation and the entrance cavern combined. The floor is concrete and way up high the ceiling looks like some kind of crinkled iron. I can't quite tell as it's so far above. The room is so vast and empty; it's mind-boggling. Although, it's not completely empty. In the distance I can see some sort of large glass machinery. Well, I think they're machines, it's hard to tell from so far away...

My body shivers and I realise how cold it is in here. I huddle my arms tightly around my body.

'Where are we?' I ask, as I continue to peer around the room.

'That is not your concern. Follow me,' Maggie says briskly. She begins walking, but I stand my ground.

'Where are you taking me?' I ask, refusing to move one more step without knowing what she has planned for me. She turns to face me, her icy stare cutting right through me. She walks back and grabs my arm roughly, pulling it and dragging me behind her.

'You'll find out soon enough,' she threatens, still holding my arm, her long, sharp nails biting into my skin.

I stumble along after her as she drags me across the room. Nerves churn in my stomach, making me feel nauseated with fear. Where the hell is she taking me? What's going to happen to me?

Maybe this wasn't such a good idea?

I watch the shapes in the distance, trying to figure out what they are. Maggie is making straight for them, so it's obvious they've got something to do with what's about to happen to me. After walking for a few minutes, I begin to register what it is I'm seeing. What I'm being taken to. I look around the room, seeing it again with fresh eyes.

I'm in a giant hangar and she's taking me on a *helicopter*.

CHAPTER TWENTY-FIVE

'I don't understand.' I stare at Maggie blankly as she continues to pull me along. She refuses to acknowledge me though. There's not even the slightest hint on her face she's even heard my question.

'How the hell do we have helicopters here?' Again my question is met with silence. They look nothing like the flying machines I've seen in old pictures and movies, but I can tell what the smooth glass spheres are used for because of the slick metal propellers that rest on top of them. No, I'm definitely not imagining them.

I shake my head, confused. It doesn't make any sense. How did they get here? Why would they even have them? What's the point?

'Maggie please,' I implore. 'What are we doing here? Where am I being taken?'

'Be quiet please!' she spits harshly at me. She tugs my arm harder and I bite down on my lip to stop myself from yelping out in pain, as her nails dig further into my skin. I slacken my body and allow myself to be pulled along. Despite my submission, she doesn't loosen her grip.

I close my eyes, trying to regain focus and control. With my eyes shut the steady, harsh clipping sound of Maggie's heels against the concrete floor becomes magnified. I can feel my heart beating faster, like the frantic wings of a caged bird. The endless ropes of knots in my stomach seem to pull tighter and my once steady legs quiver pathetically beneath me.

I try to ignore it all.

Now is not the time to be worried or scared. I've chosen to do this and I'm supposed to be feeling determined and resolute. But as much as I want to, I feel nothing of that. What was I thinking?

Panic grips my chest. I shouldn't be here. They could be taking me anywhere.

The beating of my heart intensifies. This has gone too far. I'm going to have to fess up. I need to tell her the truth.

I stop abruptly and shake my arm loose of Maggie's grip.

'I faked the test! I'm not tainted!' I cry out.

Maggie turns to look at me and the corner of her lip curls back as she peers down her nose at me.

'How stupid do you think I look?' she snarls. She grabs a hold of my arm again and jerks me back into a walk.

My heart beats faster.

'But I'm telling the truth!'

Her silence tells me everything. She doesn't believe me—of course she doesn't believe me. How many times would she have heard that one before?

Do I try to run? The hangar is so vast and empty that I quickly push that idea aside. Where would I go?

No. I'm in this now. I have to keep on going.

My eyes stray up to the roof and I wonder whether the sky is just on the other side of that corrugated iron. If there's a helicopter, it needs to get in and out somehow. I don't know whether to dance with happiness or throw up with terror at the thought of seeing the sky.

An older man greets us with a wave as we get closer to the first helicopter. He's dressed in a dark navy jumpsuit that reminds me of the army getup you'd see in old action movies. His hair is greying and the corners of his eyes are crinkled from what looks like years of laughter.

He looks over to me and winks, his eyes twinkling with mischief. I want to feel reassured by the gesture, but I'm too nervous, too suspicious. He doesn't look like he has a cruel bone in his body. Surely he wouldn't wink at me if I were about to be taken somewhere bad?

I glance back at Maggie, who still firmly grips my arm. Her demeanour is completely ruthless, and in this moment, I feel quite certain I'd be in more danger with her than with this stranger.

'Got another one for me Maggie?' the man says as we approach, jumping down from inside the helicopter. 'Surely this is some sort of record? Three in just a few weeks. I haven't seen numbers like that in years!'

'Yes Gord,' she replies, looking almost bored by the whole business.

'So this is happening?' I ask. My voice is full of fear and apprehension, but there is also a hint of excitement. I think the adrenaline must've kicked in because the thought of seeing the sky again seems to be overriding any sense of self-preservation inside of me.

'This one seems almost eager. Wish they'd all be more willing,' Gord says to Maggie, talking like I'm not even here.

I step back and look at them both.

'Where are we going?' I ask, raising my voice.

Maggie looks to Gord. 'You'll find out more when you get there,' she says. I watch her face closely, trying to see some hint of what she's hiding, but she seems uncertain. Maybe *she* doesn't even know?

'Come on kiddo.' Gord pats me on the shoulder and directs me towards the helicopter, effectively avoiding my question yet again.

I don't understand what all the secrecy is. It's not like I can go tell anyone. My feet hesitate to take another step towards the helicopter as I realise, they're taking me somewhere I don't want to go.

Gord looks so kind; I can't imagine he'd take me somewhere bad. Over his shoulder I can see Maggie standing stiffly behind him. She, on the other hand, looks like she'd be quite happy to send me off for some torment and torture.

The old man helps me into the helicopter and shows me where to sit. I'm up front with him, and Maggie thankfully isn't coming.

'Here you go kiddo.' He passes me a headset. I can feel a stupid grin on my face. I must look like a crazed person. Grinning because I'm scared, grinning because I'm eager. I'm like some lamb being led to the slaughter and I'm beaming like an idiot.

Gord begins swishing his fingers across the clear glass panel in front of him and it comes alive with digital swirling lights and indicators. I can hear the groaning of metal above as the helicopter blades start up.

'Gotta give you points kid. Most adults are a crying mess at this point, let alone the kids. Pretty much everyone requires at least some sort of sedation to relax. Sometimes they send an official or two, but they probably knew you wouldn't cause any problems.' He gives me a look of encouragement. Uncomfortable with his kindness I look back at the dashboard his fingers dart across. There are so many buttons. Gord must be incredibly smart to know what they all mean.

'You remind me a lot of the kid I had the other week. He was pretty brave, just like you,' he says after a moment.

My head whips around to look at him. He's talking about Sebastian—he has to be.

'You took the boy a few weeks ago?' I ask urgently.

'Yeah. What was his name?' He looks thoughtful for a moment. 'Ah I can't remember. Well anyhow I took him. I think he was about as eager as you are.' I'm hanging off of every word he says.

'Was his name Sebastian?' I say, hoping desperately it was.

'Well now, that might have been his name, but I couldn't be certain.' I refuse to be deflated by his uncertainty. It had to have been Sebastian. No other boys have been taken; at least not that I know of.

Plus Sebastian definitely would've been brave, no doubt about it. I just wish I could know for sure he is safe.

The hangar becomes darker, it's almost as though someone's hit the dimmer switch in here and there's a loud, whining, mechanical noise from outside of the helicopter. It's not a promising sound, in fact, it down right scares me.

'What's happening?' I yell, clutching my hands tightly around the straps across my chest.

'That'd be Maggie opening up the roof,' he replies calmly.

'What?' I throw my head back and look up through the glass body of the helicopter, up towards the receding roof. The crinkled iron slides back to reveal a gaping hole in the ceiling. The opening is dark though and I can't see anything clearly. I lean forward to try and peer around the propellers.

'Sit back kiddo. There'll be plenty of clouds for you to look at once we're flying.'

I try to do as he says and sit back, but the word 'cloud' only makes me crane my neck back even further. I can't seem to help myself. I've seen a million pictures and simulations of clouds, but can't remember ever seeing them floating far above with my own two eyes. Part of me is desperate to see them, but a more sane part of me wonders how the hell we can fly in anything even remotely similar to what I've seen on the surface televisions.

The helicopter vibrates slightly as it lifts off the ground. We're going up. Up to see the sky I never in my wildest dreams thought I'd see again. My gut clenches slightly though as I think, *but where am I being taken?*

I try to ignore the worry gnawing at my insides and only focus on the good. I'm going to see Sebastian again.

I gasp as the helicopter leaves the confines of the hangar. The desolate and barren wasteland stretches out before me. It's more terrible than it had ever seemed on the cameras. The ground is covered in a thick and dirty blanket of ice, with large, jagged cracks that snake across its endless surface. The few dead and mangled trees jut out harshly against the landscape, their limbs contorted in unnatural ways.

The sky above is even more distressing. Angry, menacing clouds roll and churn, like a fierce and ceaseless blanket that cloaks the world below. They loom over us, dark and threatening with ugly tinges of the deep purple Lysart is known for. Far in the distance there are bright flashes as violent forks of lightning descend on the forsaken earth.

There is no life out here. No way anyone could survive.

I take a peek at Gord's face. *What are we doing up here?* He looks at ease as he guides the helicopter higher, but all I can think is that he's going the wrong way.

As we continue to climb higher, the clouds envelop us and I know I am right. Higher is definitely not better. The clouds up here pummel at the small glass bubble we fly in. Like a punching bag, we are tossed and shoved to and fro across the sky.

I cower from the sight and, gripping my knees to my chest, I lower my head into them and refuse to open my eyes. Even with my eyes shut I can still feel my stomach drop with every dip the chopper takes, and I try not to whimper as my chair shudders when we take another blow.

The battering continues for the better part of an hour, but eventually it lessens and the helicopter travels more smoothly. I'm still too frightened to open my eyes though, and I keep my head tucked firmly into my knees, with my teeth clenched so tightly you'd think they were superglued together.

'It's okay,' Gord reassures me. 'The worst is over now.'

I slowly lift my head to take a look and am surprised when my eyes meet a searing light. I take several heavy blinks in an attempt to see better, and squint as I try to adjust to the brightness that surrounds me.

My vision gradually clears, and when I realise what I can see I gasp and press my hands up against the glass. The vicious clouds no longer surround us and we're wrapped in the bright, white luminescence of soft, fluffy clouds.

I'm surrounded by the things of fairy tales and daydreams. The clouds you spend a lifetime imagining when asked what heaven looks like.

My eyes dart up, down and all around as I watch the bulbous shapes emerge and then disappear as we move through them. They look so impressive and solid from the distance, but up close they are just wisps of air.

After a while my eyes start becoming sore. I'm constantly rubbing them, or having to close them, or take long blinks. There's a whole lot of bright white out there.

I hear Gord chuckling.

'What's the matter?' he laughs.

'They're a lot brighter than I thought,' I say. 'Not that I'm complaining! I'll take sore eyes any day to see these clouds.'

My gobsmacked wonder at the clouds is just beginning to wear off, and my feelings of anxiety resurface, when the helicopter breaks through the mist. I squeal and jump forwards with excitement.

'The sun,' I yell to Gord. 'That's the sun!' I repeat, pointing at the large bright ball of light and bouncing on my seat. I'm almost quivering with delight.

The most amazing blue sky is overhead and a blanket of clouds lies below. The sun is bright and piercing, it's near impossible to look at straight on. I already feel warmer as its glow shines down on my skin, and my expression is one of total awe. I never thought I'd see the sun again.

'Ahh that never gets old,' Gord says. I try to imagine countless people seeing the sun for the first time in so long. It must be amazing constantly getting to witness their joy.

'Where are we going?' I ask Gord seriously, as we pass through another thick cloud.

'I was wondering when you'd get to asking me again. I'm surprised you waited this long to be honest.' He takes a deep breath before he continues. 'The reason I didn't tell you before, in the hangar, is because Maggie is part of the ARC society. She's not tainted so she doesn't know about where we take you.

'I'm not certain what she thinks happens, but I'm fairly certain she assumes it's somewhere pretty terrible. It probably doesn't help that I'm not at liberty to discuss what happens when she's around. It should be fine to tell you now though.'

'Okay,' I respond slowly. His explanation makes sense but it doesn't give any indication of whether I'm being taken somewhere good or bad.

'So where I'm taking you, there are other people like you. Special people. You've grown up calling them the tainted, but there's nothing wrong with them at all. In fact people who are tainted are rather extraordinary. And you're one of them.' He looks at me in a way that tells me I should feel encouraged by what he's said, but all I can think is, *what have I got myself into?*

'They'll explain all of this in more detail when we get there. In short, I'm taking you somewhere where you don't need to be afraid to be yourself.'

I turn away from Gord and stare out at the horizon. It doesn't sound bad, in fact it almost sounds welcoming. I just don't know how I'm going to fit in. Being tainted has always been a bad thing. How am I supposed to change the beliefs that have been encouraged my entire life?

Something in the distance glints and the sharp, bright reflection catches my eye. I lean forward in my seat and squint my eyes in an attempt to make out the shiny object.

'What's that up ahead?'

'That's Hope City,' says Gord. 'Your new home.' As we get closer to the tall crystalline structures in the distance they become clearer.

'But it's ... well it's ... is it above ground?' I stammer.

'Yes.'

'But what about the impact winter?' I ask, my words racing over each other.

'It started to recede here about five years ago,' he answers patiently. I sit back in my seat, shocked. I never expected to see the sun again, let alone imagine the possibility of living under it.

I lean forward again trying to discern what exactly lies below. Through the wispy clouds pulled thin like candy floss, I can see a blinding white reflection of the sun dancing along the desolate waste of ice that still extends below us. The vast sheet stretches away from the city, for miles into the distance.

As we get closer though, the ice gradually stops and is replaced by large, empty fields of green and brown that are wild with untamed growth. The long grass ripples as the wind whips across the open fields. It seems to thrive in the flat expanse between the ice and the city.

I focus ahead on the large structures that reach for the sky. The sun seems to reflect blindingly from their surfaces and the buildings are so close to one another they appear to be all connected.

'It's so big. How did they build it so fast?'

'Well most of it was here before. This was once a city. So it didn't take too much effort to get it running again once the ice began to recede.'

As the helicopter lowers further and enters the city's maze of buildings I start to see the shapes of people on the streets far below. They're so tiny from this far away and there are so many of them that I begin to worry. In a place so big with so many people, how am I going to find Sebastian?

I grip my pendant tightly in one hand and try to take a steadying breath. Finding just one person in the masses that crowd this endless web of streets and buildings will be impossible.

'Okay we'll be landing shortly.' Gord says it kindly, but instead of feeling encouraged, I feel crippled by nerves. What the hell am I doing? What have I been thinking? *But more importantly, what's about to happen to me?*

I turn to Gord.

'Are you tainted?' I ask. Hoping desperately he is. That he's proof nothing bad happens to people who've been taken. That things are not about to get worse.

He looks at me knowingly. 'No,' he responds. 'I'm talented.'

~

END OF BOOK ONE

~

Continue in book 2: Talented
Available here!

ACKNOWLEDGMENTS

My first, and most important, thank you is to you, the reader. It means the world to me to have people take the time to read my work, and I hope I made it worth your while.

Thank you to all the people who helped make *Tainted* happen. This was a task I definitely couldn't have accomplished alone.

Pete, who spent endless hours providing me with his amazing editing skills, encouragement and advice in helping to bring *Tainted* to life, I couldn't have done this without you.

To my mum who gave me so much sound advice about writing and who is probably the loudest, most enthusiastic member of my own personal cheer squad. Without her help I'd probably still be stuck on the third chapter.

Thank you to my dad, who helped me with his ridiculous general knowledge of how things work. It helped me immensely with both creating and understanding the world I built.

To Jen, whose time is generally under siege by her cohort of rugrats, thank you for dedicating some of your precious free time to *Tainted*. You provided me with so many new ideas to make Elle's journey more exciting and your input really helped make the world come alive.

Finally, to Hen who has lent her beautiful face to the cover of this novel. Your never-ending support gives me the courage to pursue my dreams and I can't thank you enough.

This book is better because of all of your input and I'm so grateful to everyone who helped me make it the book it is today.

It's one thing to have words down on a page, but something else entirely to have people who support your writing and believe in those words. So thank you guys!

ALSO BY ALEXANDRA MOODY

The Liftsal Guardians Series

The Liftsal Guardians

The Brakys' Lair

The Oblivion Stone

The Rift War

The ARC series

Tainted

Talented

Fractured

Destined

ABOUT THE AUTHOR

ALEXANDRA MOODY is an Australian author. She studied Law and Commerce in her hometown, Adelaide, before going on to spend several years living abroad in Canada and the UK. She is a serious dog-lover, double-black-diamond snowboarder and has a love/hate relationship with the gym.

Never miss a release!
Sign up at: www.subscribepage.com/TheARCsubscribe

For more information:

www.alexandramoody.com
info@alexandramoody.com